Penguin Books

Penguin Modern Stories 5

D0481072

Penguin
Modern
Stories 5

Edited by Judith Burnley

Penguin Books

Penguin Books Ltd, Harmondsworth,
Middlesex, England
Penguin Books Australia Ltd, Ringwood,
Victoria, Australia

First published in book form in Great Britain by Penguin Books 1970

The stories by Penelope Gilliatt titled *The Last to go* (1969),
Property, *An Antique Love Story*, and *Foreigners*, (1970)
copyright ©, in the respective years shown, by
the New Yorker Magazine Inc.,
'A Ball of Malt and Madame Butterfly' © Benedict Kiely, 1970

'Babyface'; 'Don't Shoot' © Andrew Travers, 1970
'Crrrrrrrkkkkkkk'; 'Mister Newcome Runs for the 8.35 a.m.' © Anthony
Burton, 1970

Made and printed in Great Britain by
C. Nicholls & Company Ltd, Philips Park Press, Manchester
Set in Monotype Baskerville

Contents

All the stories in this volume are published here for the first time
in this country.

Foreigners

'Oh god, I wish the shops were open,' said the great atheist economist, near tears, to his terror. It was an ice-cold June Sunday. He had eaten roast mutton and apple charlotte. Three people in his Wiltshire drawing-room slept, and so did his dogs. He looked at the fire hard enough to dry out his eyeballs, or perhaps to singe them.

'Sundays are impossible. I can't stand Sundays,' his voice said, again frightening him. The voice was shouting. His hands were shaking. Sunday lunch, sleep; radio, muffins, sleep; gin-and-lime, the cold roast, radio, sleep. His English life, his English wife. On the opposite side of their English fireplace Sara was answering letters on her headed English note cards: 'Mrs Thomas Flitch, The Dower House.' And so on and so on. His Indian mother was in a wheelchair by the bay window, reading. The sight of her brought back some Sunday in India. Himself a child on a bicycle. Dusk, nearly dark. Groups of young men sitting on the ground near a closed library, reading and talking by the light of flares in petrol cans.

His stepson, Simon, a tall stockbroker, guffawed for no obvious reason and kicked the chin of a sleeping dog off a pile of Thomas's books, although he didn't go on to pick up any of the books.

'It'll be Monday all too soon,' Sara said, with the brotherly grimness that he had learned to read in her as a style of intimacy. Now she was doing household accounts and checking the milk bill. She looked fatigued and drawn.

He loved her, and wished to save her the frightful inroads of Anglo-Saxon activity, and hated her hat. She was still wearing the ugly straw that she had put on for morning church. She had cooked the lunch in it. Thomas liked her hair and loathed all her hats. In fifty-odd years of high regard for Englishwomen and awe of the fortitude and grace he saw in them, he had never accepted their defiling hats.

Simon's daughter, Pippa, a beauty of six who had one blue and one green eye, swarmed watchfully into the room on her stomach with Thomas's encouragement and bounced up with a Red Indian war cry behind the chairs of two sleeping visitors. So she was as oppressed by Sunday as he was. He admired her for dealing with it capably. There was an interlude of chaos. A pot of coffee was spilled, and Sara had to get a damp cloth for the trousers of one of the visitors, who was involved in an unwise pretence that he hadn't actually been asleep. Thomas seemed to be seeing things through the wrong end of a telescope. People appeared to be very small, and their voices were too loud for their size. Pippa was much scolded.

'I've brought something for Great-granny,' she said several times, while the storm went on around her pig-tailed head and finally spent itself. She heard her father and Sara out, and meanwhile held the present in her closed hand.

After five minutes, Simon attended to what she was saying and assumed a look of astuteness. 'Have you got something in your hand?' he asked. Pause. 'Something for Great-granny?' he carried on shrewdly. 'Let's have a look at it, in case it's one of the things Great-granny doesn't eat.' He tried to force open her fingers. 'Let Daddy tell you. You're old enough to know by now that in the country where Great-granny comes from they don't eat some of the things we eat. It's not that they're fussy, it's because they think it's wrong. You know that now, don't you, Pippa?'

'You told me before,' said Pippa.

'Ah, yes, you see; it's a chocolate. So we're all right. I

thought so. Why didn't you show it to me in the first place? Run and give it to Great-granny,' he said, some time after Pippa was already there. 'Granny, Pippa's brought you a special chocolate,' he went on, some time after the old lady had thanked the child.

Thomas's mother was named Arathra Chib. Although his father had acknowledged the son in due time – when the boy grew up to be phenomenally educable – he had never married Miss Chib. She had stayed in a Delhi shack made of biscuit tins and a tarpaulin. Mr Flitch, not a bad man, had worked most of his life in India in the tea business. When his bastard turned out to be studious, the boy was accepted into the English bachelor's house for a short time before he was shipped off to prep school and public school in his father's country. He spent the holidays in England with any parents who would have him. If nothing worked out, he lived in the empty school. Some master, equally lonely, would be set to giving him extra essays and physical training to keep him occupied. Thomas bore England no grudge for the youth it dealt him. On the contrary. After getting a double first at Oxford he married Sara, scarcely able to believe his luck. She was a pretty young widow with a small son, and Thomas went to law to give the little boy his own surname.

'Well done, Pippa. Chocolates are perfectly safe,' Simon said laboriously in the direction of the wheelchair.

Thomas was already in the grip of a disorder not at all native to him, and now he suddenly confounded everything he believed he felt for Simon by remembering with hatred one of his adopted son's practical jokes. Some like Sunday long ago, the child Simon had crept up to his Indian step-grandmother when she was asleep in the same wheelchair and thrown a blanket over her, shouting that she was a canary in a cage. Thomas had kept the memory at arm's length until now, when it occurred to him that Simon's sensibility had not much changed. The insight cracked Thomas's heart slightly before he got rid of it again.

His mother's vegetarianism had been carefully respected

9

at lunch, with the usual faint suggestion that it was aberrant and therefore embarrassing, although Sara did try to conceal her opinion. Before the apple charlotte, Miss Chib was given a bowl of pea soup with a spoonful of whipped cream in it. Thomas had noticed the cream, which represented effort. It also represented licence, an unusual small expense on a treat beyond the necessities of Sara's food budget. Though Thomas was greatly revered he had never been well off, and now that he had retired from government advisory jobs he earned nothing much except by writing. Simon, who was well on his way to becoming a millionaire through his dealings on the stock exchange, had leaned over his pleasant young wife to peer at his step-grandmother's plate. 'I say,' he said jovially, 'I see my mama's been lashing out a bit.'

Thomas's house, which he could barely keep up, was run mostly on the income from a small chain of modern toy shops that he had built up for his wife over the years. He had given her the capital for the first one on their twentieth wedding anniversary, when he had already bought a Georgian pendant that he dearly wished her to have; but he had asked her what she would like before he gave it to her, and she told him. She had ideas about how a toy shop should be run in these times. Strong plastics, instructive building sets, things that would save women trouble. After a long while of keeping the pendant hidden and unlooked at in his sock drawer, Thomas had to bring himself to hunt for someone to buy it back, for he couldn't afford both presents. He got nothing like the price of it. But Sara's idea had obviously been the better one, he told himself, though without believing a word of it, for where would they all be now without Mama's business venture, as his stepson warmly pointed out to him on a walk round the garden this afternoon.

'Why don't you let me take over the accounts?' Simon said.

'What accounts?' Thomas asked, sheltering in slow-wittedness. He seemed to be fending something off. Nothing he was doing was like himself, and Simon looked at him oddly before poking a black pig in the belly.

'You should keep more pigs and run the place as a farm,' Simon said. 'And all this could be ploughed up, too.' He gestured across the lawn that ran down to a stream and then up again to his own cottage, which Thomas had given him as a wedding present. 'The expenses of this place are ridiculous. Mama's a Trojan but she's looking pretty whacked.'

'She needs more help. I must see about more help.'

'As I say, I could do the papers of the business. You wear yourself out with them.'

'They seem to be taking longer at the moment. You wouldn't have time.'

'Oh, I could do them on the train to the City some morning every week.'

That fast? He probably could.

Simon looked around at the bigger house with an alert eye. 'This place is potentially a gold mine. It's madness to run it as a private house. If you turned it into a business, you could keep six maids and gardeners if you wanted and write them off against the pigs. Or whatever else you went in for. Mama's been talking of sugar beet.'

Sugar beet? Sugar beet hadn't come up. Thomas steadied his eyes on the Tudor stable yard and his library window. 'I won't have it,' he said, shaking.

'Buck up, Father. Nobody thinks it's your fault. You're one of the world's thinkers. Been doing much writing?'

Thomas lied, against his temperament. 'Quite a bit.' Pause. 'Preliminaries.' Oh, come off it. But the ground seemed to be moving away. He felt as if Simon were lifting him by the collar and dangling him so that his feet were off the earth and his toes straining to reach something. Simon's big head and loose mouth loomed above him against the ridiculous English summer sky, which was the colour of iron.

'Your last book was very impressive,' Simon said. 'Prunella and I both thought so. Reflected glow, you know.'

He blew his nose on a red spotted handkerchief that he wore in yeoman moods. 'A bit above my level, I'm afraid, some of it.'

'Oh dear. Was it hard to follow?' Thomas asked, taking him to mean what he said. 'Which passages?' But Simon had never got beyond page twenty-seven, and after that he had merely left the book out in case his mother and stepfather came unexpectedly for drinks. So now he was at a disadvantage, which angered him, and he lost sight of the gratitude he usually summoned up for the stepfather who had spent much of his life obliging his adopted son's ambitions for parents with a big house and a dashing car. At many moments of weakness, or love, Thomas had spent far more money than he could afford or even wished for the sake of Simon's joy in the holidays. The days when he could do it, or would, were now over. Their town house had been sold, lingeringly, with rearguard modernizing actions to keep up its price. The eventual loss kept Thomas awake at night. For the present, in the daytime, he was abruptly fed up with the whole lot: with himself, his insufficiency, the toll that his financial state seemed to be taking of his wife, and the colossally polite head of his stepson, which was hanging over him now as if it had a miniature keg of brandy around its neck.

'Men are not made better by calamity,' he said. At the same time he was engaged in disliking his own state of intellect at the moment, which appeared to own no responsibility for the production of that sentence and buzzed around small problems without much resource or repose.

'What's that from? Is it an Indian saying?'

'What? No. Where was she thinking of putting the sugar beet?'

'Hey, I say, chin up. No calamity in this house, eh? Mama's full of beans.'

'She's very tired.'

'Take her to the sun. Take her to Greece. A friend of mine's got a yacht. You could charter it.'

'It would be rather ludicrous.' When we can't afford someone to clean the house, Thomas added silently.

'I could do it on the firm and it wouldn't cost anybody anything. A conference yacht.' Simon laughed loudly. 'Mama could be entertaining foreign buyers. I do think you should let me go into the pigs.'

Thomas told Simon to leave. He said he had work to do. Simon walked down to the stream and across the bridge to his own cottage, waving with his usual cordiality, which was unfailing because it depended on no cordial impulse. Thomas came back past the drawing-room. He could see his mother, playing with Pippa, and his wife talking to a woman friend by the window. Sara smiled at him. Thomas looked at them all, and then at Simon, who was now a small figure and in another sense no longer monstrous because he was walking exactly as he had done when he was a very young child and most moving to Thomas, with his hands in his pockets and his back arched. The familiarity of everyone eased the strangeness in Thomas's head. I wish I had them all here, he thought. I wish we were together. I wish we were having a picnic, and that it was hot, and I do indeed wish that we were all together; though even if I were to hold the whole world against my chest, it would probably save us from very little. The longing was unaccustomed. He came to the drawing-room window, which was open. His mind had at last found its way back to its usual cast when he heard Sara's friend talking to her.

'... start bestirring himself, for heaven's sake. Leaving you to do everything. What's a brilliant mind –'

'He is brilliant, that's so,' Sara said over her. 'But he's never made the career he could have done. He won't use his elbows.'

But I am not that man, Thomas thought, shivering in a heap on the flower bed where he had dropped on to all fours so as not to be seen. I am not that man, he thought again, straightening up now, for in the next instant it seemed entirely necessary that he should not hide, should visibly walk to the front door and into his library. I will not be that man. He sat behind his desk for a long time, skipping Sunday's cold mutton supper, rousing himself to say good-bye to the visitors, trying to deal with the paper-work of Sara's business. Wholesale and retail prices, markups, running expenses, employment insurance. Nausea. Sara, beautiful Sara, appeared in the accounts as the manageress. Deductible, to be candid. No. Once not. She had left samples of toys and plastic playthings among his books and manuscripts. Garbage. Her piercing household face swam across his eyeline, even more changed from its former self than now, and hermetic in its enthusiasm for nursery objects properly researched by child psychiatrists to be fit for the middle-class children who would lose them without a pang. There was a pale-pink celluloid rattle on his desk. It was decorated with an overdressed pale-blue rabbit in non-toxic paint. Long ago, he had found Simon a Hindu rattle made of chased silver with an ivory handle shaped for a child to hold. *What shall we leave behind us?* he thought. He stared at a Rajput scene on the wall among his books. 'Won't use his elbows.' I know as little of love as I do of painting, he thought. The days of smoking a pipe sud-denly came back to him, and he realized that he was biting down on his own teeth. His mind seemed to be acting like mercury. He saw it slipping around in a pool and then dividing into drops that ran apart. He leaned back often for a rest and once he got up to type an envelope on an old typewriter in the window. The typewriter had been made in Delhi many years ago, copied from an English Underwood that had been reproduced in every detail except for the vital spring to drive the keys back. In the machine's heyday the deficiency had not been regarded as crippling. Labour was cheap, time ran slow, and a girl sat beside the man typist to return each key by hand as he pressed it. Thomas had grown up in the neighbourhood of the machine and one day he had bought it, bringing it to England by boat and vaguely intending to explore the possibility of supplying a spring, though he also liked it well as it still was.

He delayed going upstairs for as long as possible, partly

in a hopeless pretence of getting the papers finished with, and partly to avoid Sara. But she was lying awake. He guessed her to be worrying about money. Temper defeated pity and he attacked her rabidly for, of all things, going to her Anglican church. It appeared to him suddenly that there was a link between her flouted ambition for him and the ethic of a religion more alien to his own thought than he had ever dreamed. He sounded to himself like some tendentious student with balloon words coming out of his mouth.

'Jesus was the first Catholic and therefore the first Mr Success of the profit motive,' he said, putting on his dressing-gown and feeling foolish. 'Christianity and capitalism are inseparable. Why do you go? Why do you spoil Sundays?'

Sara said, 'You're not well. You're losing your grip.' She watched him quite carefully.

'I daresay. We can't stay in this house. We simply can't keep it up.'

She was quiet.

So he snarled. 'Does it mean that much to you?'

'What do you think?' Now the rage poured out: All these years, our things, deserve, owe, our time of life, everything we've been through.

Help, he thought. I can't go on. I can't manage any of it.

Earn, she threw at him.

Relearn, he thought, adding the first three letters to her word in his head as if they were playing a game. 'Church!' he shouted.

'You never shout,' she said, staring at him.

'You spoil Sundays!'

'Socrates was the first man who thought about thinking,' she said, sitting on the window seat and surprising him in every way.

'Uh?' he said over her.

'Jesus may have been the first man who understood the power of some actions. The power of forgiving an enemy, for instance.'

'You mean me, don't you?' He held his head.

On Monday, when Sara had left the house early to see to things in two of the toy shops on the other side of the county, he could find nothing at home that he felt up to doing. He drove himself to a café in the nearby market town and simply listened to pacify himself. It was a teashop, with one half that sold honey and home-made scones and a second half with tables where the walls were decorated with a mixture of horse brasses and psychedelic posters. One of the middle-aged women who kept the shop had ordered a set of posters about the Paris rising of May 1968 because she had gone to the Sorbonne to study when she was a girl. The teashop was next door to one of Sara's branches. Remorse had drawn Thomas there and kept him pinned, though he was also wild for flight. An arthritic woman came into the café, alone, with a paper bag carrying the name of Sara's shop.

'You feel safer at home than what you do further away,' she said after a long silence, addressing no one. 'Further away you might be a nuisance.'

Unplaced impatience felt like burrs on Thomas's skin. He leaned over to her and said, 'No, you should get out,' which affronted her. He had broken the fourth wall.

In the late afternoon, slow to go home, he dropped in on an elderly doctor friend and played tennis. His hands shook and his friend prescribed a sedative.

'Work a strain at the minute?' said the doctor, watching.

'That sort of thing.'

'Take two a day,' said the doctor. 'Sleeping all right?' The whole circumstance startled him. He expected limitless serenity of a man half-Indian, and indeed Thomas had sustained the expectation for twenty years or more.

'Mostly,' Thomas said.

'Let me know. Keep in touch.'

'I can't concentrate. I don't understand myself. Sara's being a brick.'

'Your English is more English than mine,' the doctor said,

Foreigners

not really to make conversation but to find more time to see. Thomas's mind seemed to be elsewhere, and there was no perfunctory laugh in return.

The doctor was concerned enough about him to trail him on a journey that Thomas then made to London airport. He merely sat at the coffee counter there, hour after hour, alone. The talk of strangers alleviated something. At one point he inquired at the Air India desk and made a booking. Then he went back to the coffee counter, where two girls were talking about pop singers.

'I wouldn't mind marrying Paul,' said the blonde girl of the pair. She had a beautifully high forehead and an upper lip that twitched softly, like a cow's in a fly-ridden summer.

'Paul?' said her freckled friend. 'Ringo any day.'

'I think Paul's sweet.'

'Ringo's more of a husband. More masterful.'

'Well, if you're talking about *masterful*,' the blonde said vaguely.

'Don't you want to be mastered?'

'Not much.'

'I don't think a marriage with Ringo would work if he wasn't the master.'

'There's always divorce.'

They paused, and then the freckled girl said, 'What about the cooking? I can't see me cooking.'

'I wouldn't mind doing Paul a steak,' said the blonde. 'Or spaghetti. As long as it wasn't fish with the eyes left in, or a chicken. Not a whole chicken. Nothing with innards.'

'Would you look after him if he was ill? That's what I'd have to do for Ringo, you know. I wouldn't mind. I should think he'd be very demanding. Anyone in the public eye.'

'Paul's kept his sincerity. He's not spoilt.'

Thomas quietly bought them another cup of coffee each, and they giggled when they realized it and clinked the thick coffee mugs with him before carrying on with their conversation as is he weren't there.

'What sort of ill, anyway?' said the blonde.

'Sick, say,' said freckles.

Thomas saw Sara in his mind's eye. She was never ill, but now she looked beaten and angered by something he must be doing to her. For richer, for poorer.

'What sort of sick? English sick or American sick?' said the blonde.

'What's the difference, then?'

'Cor, don't you know that? American sick is just ill. When they mean English sick, they say throw-up sick or sick to your stomach.'

'English sick.'

'Come to think of it, I'd look after him anyway. So long as he didn't carry on about it. You wouldn't catch Paul carrying on.'

They ran for their plane, thanking Thomas for the coffee. He missed them and paced around and made another booking at the Air India counter, stalling grandly about actually buying the ticket without even noticing that the people on duty were the ones who had humoured him before. After a time, his doctor friend had seen enough of his extremity and took him for a drink in the airport bar.

'Funny, meeting you,' Thomas said, refusing any ordinary guess that it could be no accident.

'Off somewhere?' said the doctor.

Thomas suddenly started to shake so badly that the ice in his glass chattered. He fished the cubes out and put them into an ashtray and found it all he could do not to weep at the mess they made with the ash.

'You need help,' his friend said.

'What for?' Thomas said. 'The pills will do the trick. It's mostly that I can't sleep.'

'There are things that pills don't do so well as a rest and treatment. You need proper rest.'

A county hospital treated Thomas that week for acute depression. He was greatly humiliated. He was also in fear. To the family, who were breezy, referring to 'Daddy's trouble', he revealed nothing. Sara drove him scornfully to the hospital three times a week, for he wasn't supposed to drive. This on top of everything else, she seemed to be thinking, although she did everything she might to eliminate exhaustion and scorn from her voice. On the car journey, which took an hour and a half each way, he talked to her with all the will he could muster about the toy shops. It was barely manageable. He found it impossible to believe that he had ever been able to write a book, or give a lecture, or advise a government. Other scholars heard that he was unwell and sent him notes made remote by their instinct that his straits must mortify him. Sara felt many things, including affection, balked control, trouble over his loss of weight, and enmity towards one of the weak. Sometimes she tried talking to him about India, with a genuine impulse to do what she could. She did not feel shame, or any sense of partaking in the very view of life that was nearly extinguishing him.

At the end of the hospital treatment they went away to the Caribbean on holiday, by an aeroplane that belonged to a director of Simon's firm. An old friend of Thomas's lived on the island, but he was a Black politician with a mind in the world that Thomas had lost for the moment. Sara had letters to people who owned polo ponies and valuable land for development. So Thomas played bridge with them, and swam, and learned to use aqualungs. He began to feel like a king, more or less. Or fit, at the least. One day he slipped off alone, out of interest, to look up a local doctor who took him on a tour of hospitals. Maternity wards with two women to a bed. Children with rickets. He didn't tell Sara much of it.

When they got back to England, Simon had a surprise waiting. He had exchanged houses with them. Sara and Thomas were to be in the cottage, and Simon's household of three in Thomas's place. The point was the running expenses. Most of the move had been accomplished already. Sara knew of it. 'We didn't tell you because you were too ill,' she said. 'We decided to wait so that there was a secret for you when you came back. When you were your old self.'

'It's a fine idea,' Thomas said to her, expounding it to himself and meantime walking around Simon's cottage with resentment for every stone of the place. 'They're an expanding family. There's less work for you to do here. It's very good of him. Where will I work?'

'I thought you'd be relieved. The financial burden. Young shoulders. Besides, he can write a lot of it off against tax, you know. So it's better in every way.'

(*Where will I work?*)

'It's very good of him,' he said, going across to the window to look at their house and then turning away in pain. He went on to bump his head on a beam. His state of mind was so much lighter than before that he laughed. 'If *I* hit my head, at five foot nine, no wonder Simon wanted to switch,' he said.

'It has nothing to do with his height,' Sara said stiffly.

The only things left to be moved were Thomas's books. The Sunday after they came back from the West Indies, he and Sara and his mother – who was living with them now in a room not much larger than a cupboard, although the view, as Simon constantly said, was staggering – went formally to lunch in their old house. Sara started off in her hat, left on from church.

'For heaven's sake, take your hat off,' Thomas said.

'Do you need one of your pills, dear?'

'No, I just hate your hat. We're going to our own house, aren't we? We're not going out.'

'We are going out. You've got to adjust. The doctor said that about the income.' This was the way she spoke of it: 'The income.' She meant his earnings, not the yield of the toy-shop business, but she had never been in the habit of referring to them so distinctly, let alone to the fact that they were thin on the ground at the moment. 'We are going out. We're lunching with Simon and Prunella in their new home.'

He threw a bottleful of his pills into the kitchen sink and tried to get them to go down the drain with the handle of a dish mop. 'I hate the word "home",' he said. 'It's like "doggy". The place is a house.'

'It is my language,' Sara said. She saw then that she had been unpardonable, but the odd thing was that he did pardon her, and laughed, and quietly fished some of the soggy pills out of the sink in case he fancied one later after all.

Simon was sitting in Thomas's armchair, which was too big to be moved to the cottage. Prunella had nicely been trying to prise him out of it before they came, but she was timid of him. 'Better not to make an issue of it by my shifting,' Simon said. 'No need to treat him like an invalid.'

At lunch, where there were maids to serve, Sara kept watching Thomas's plate. 'Eat up,' she said when he left something.

'No, thanks.'

'The stomach shrinks. He's doing very well. He's put on six pounds,' she told the table. She looked splendid herself, said the table. She did. But it seemed to Thomas that she was too doughty for him, somehow, and the hat finished it. For years and years, her frailer beauty had made him feel physically famished for her, but he had generally subdued the longing because she seemed worn out with housework. And now she was as strong as a carthorse, and he didn't give a damn. He suddenly felt farcically drawn to Simon's Prunella, which seemed a sign of health if nothing else.

'What's the joke?' Prunella said gently.

'There's a Russian story about a peasant who dreams night after night of having a bowl of cherry jam and no spoon to eat it with. And then at last he goes to bed with a spoon, and he doesn't dream.'

Simon poured some port into the Stilton and talked of a hot tip about buying shares in a firm called Gas Purification Enterprises Limited. Thomas got up eventually from his new place in the middle of the table, which he had quite liked because it had leg access to a rung where he could wriggle his feet when he was bored. He went to his old library, and Pippa followed him, equally enlivened to leave.

'Would you like to see my filthy sculptures?' she said.

'Very much,' he said.

'They're in your library.' They were made in Plasticine, and obviously based on photographs of Hindu sculpture in the art books on his bottom shelves. The six-year-old instinct had made them curiously abstract, and Thomas was much moved. The two were poring over them when Simon came into the room. He absorbed the little grey figures in a few seconds and his face bulged. He left the library and came back with a riding crop. Thomas found it hard to believe. He tried to block things, but they went fast. The little girl was held by the back of her bent neck and the thong of the crop swished down on to her cotton dress. When Thomas tried to grab the child away, the lash caught him in the eye.

'Stop!' he shouted, reaching again for the child and closing his red-hot eye.

'You speak of stopping,' said Simon. 'You led her on. Five, six, seven.' It went on to nine before Thomas put an end to it. Simon by then had heavily said, 'This hurts me more than it hurts you' to Pippa, and when the chaos was over Thomas began to laugh, for the lash of the crop literally had curled round on to Simon's back between each stroke and it had broken some skin, though the man was too excited to notice it. Picking up the child, who was breathing in gulps like an oarsman at the end of a race, Thomas bent down to save her sculptures and carried her through to her mother. 'I want these kept always,' he said, thrusting the figures at her face.

'What are they?'

'They're sculptures of Pippa's. They're to be kept in my library. My books are to stay, too. I have a lot of work to do and there isn't enough room in the other place.'

Sara said, 'What was all that noise?' She looked more closely at the figures and turned away from him.

'What is it?' he said, watching her and flooded by a feeling that he had not expected. 'You're not weeping?'

'You don't seem to be any better than before.' She bent a

little to lean her fists on the window seat, with her back to him. 'You're not trying. You give in to these wilful tempers. You're not yourself. I've got more than enough to do. You were never like this.'

'Well, I am now. Simon beat Pippa for these.'

'No wonder.'

'He'd better have beaten me.' Sara swung round and Thomas was half touched by the horror in her. 'She must have liked a book of mine,' he said.

'They're in that wretched old-fashioned Plasticine,' she went on, switching ground and speaking as if that compounded things. 'Who could have given it to her? Prunella and I are so careful. She has plenty of the proper sort.'

'This kind smells nice,' he said.

'One of the *points* about the new kind is that it's odourless.'

'Smell!' he shouted. 'Not "odour." You even take away smells. Actually, I think I probably gave her the clay.'

'But we don't stock it.'

'No, I got it from an art shop.' In Sara's canon this was perfidy. She looked betrayed, and tight around the chin. 'You'll have to put up with it, darling,' he said gaily, refusing to fall in with her mood.

There was a pause while Sara collected herself, and then she said they must go back and do the accounts.

'I've some work to do,' he said.

'Yes, we have.'

'No, my own work.'

'In that case there are all the books to move.'

'I'll go on with it here. There's more space.'

'Have you asked Simon?'

'Why the hell should I ask Simon?'

A dam burst again: All he's done for you. (Prunella left the room.) Picking up the pieces of your life for you. A foreigner accepted as if you were his own father. No real son could have done more. Difficult times for everyone. Your trouble. Everyone under great strain. You didn't mean. The subject of Pippa better not discussed (and then discussed at length). It occurred to Thomas as he listened to her that Sara had not changed a whit in the whole time they had been married. No hint or taint of him had touched her. She had remained her strong English self, and in truth she did put up with a good deal, for in her terms a scholar's life must always have stood for a life of privation, which would explain the furious resolve that clenched the lines in her face. All the same, he had work to do.

'Before you leave, you'd better apologize to Simon,' she said. He left the room, picking up the little erotic figures and locking them into his desk drawer.

Sara followed him. 'What are you doing?' she said.

'Nothing,' he said.

'What are you thinking about?' She pursued him.

'Nothing,' he said again, smiling at her, for she was Sara. ('Remember the nine tenets of resistance in a country occupied by foreign forces,' he said to himself. ' "We know nothing, we recognize nothing, we give nothing, we are capable of nothing, we understand nothing, we sell nothing, we help nothing, we reveal nothing, we forget nothing.' ")

'Doesn't it hurt your pride? It must,' she said, not unkindly but in a rare and urgent search for a response of any sort at all.

After contemplation, he replied quite seriously, 'A little. Very little. At first. Not now. I think it's harder on you.'

'You've never been properly recognized.'

'You mean well paid.' He waited. 'To choose to do the work one wants, I suppose one will quite often have to renounce the idea of making a fortune. Yes? I'm sorry, my dear.' A few minutes before, he had tried to add 'We apologize for nothing' to the rules in his head, but he knew that Sara would always move him to compunction.

Alone then in his library, feeling fine, his spirits began to mount. He thought about some work, and also about the world, as he had not since he was in India. The sense of being part of a general flux had been lost for years. There grew in him a wish to touch with his fingers a future that he knew was that of many others. The disorder that had seemed to him for decades to determine the course of events regrouped itself like a pile of iron filings suddenly organized by a magnet, and in a flash of optimism it appeared quite possible that men in the days to come might wish to find out more than concerned them at the moment. Probably this curiosity will be quite superficial, he thought to himself, as it is in me until I have more time to spend on it. But it will be better. He considered for several hours, making notes and getting up now and then for books. He felt he had his hand on a way to proceed, and one that might be of some consequence, with luck. Simon's heavy tread moved about upstairs and his voice shouted something at a maid. He was calling for a sherry. 'And a tonic water with ice for Mr Flitch in the library. No gin. He doesn't drink. Remember that. Pru, he is still here, isn't he? He hasn't drifted back to his own place yet, eh? Do you think we have to offer him a meal?'

Thomas looked out of the window. I'll leap into my life, he thought, if it splits my face to bits.

Penelope Gilliatt

Property

PEG
MAX
ABBERLEY

An arc of pale sand-coloured hessian reaching around stage and from floor to beyond eye-view. Three single beds, pinned to floor, equidistant. Iron bedsteads, extremely beautiful. Beige and dark brown blankets, white linen. Small antique tables in polished dark woods beside each character, stacked with belongings. ABBERLEY'S *with piles of cigarettes, notepads, lawyer's folders, photographs, a torch, pencils, jar of caramels.* MAX'S *with a pipe, tobacco, scientific journals.* PEG'S, *notably more bare, with a few books, playing cards, jar of caramels. All have bottles of pills, booze, glasses, thermoses, radios and earphones. At the bottom of each bed there appears to be a miniature* TV, *facing the people lying on the beds. The machines are actually electrocardiographs. The wires recording from the characters' forearms and calves are not particularly visible for the time being. Characters not in nightclothes. Dressed to be ready at any time for expeditions and undertakings that will not actually occur.* PEG *in a grey and white print and some soft turban or scarf that hides her hair.* ABBERLEY *in white shirt, city tie, black trousers.* MAX *in grey flannel trousers and grey brawny pullover. Bare feet. Shoes and socks by beds, neat. No other furniture. All characters are youngish and healthy. Spotlights trained on their beds represent reading lamps. When a character goes to sleep or withdraws from contact, his spotlight snaps off.*

There is also a perpetual faint natural light in this space where they live immovably together.

4.45 a.m. Curtain up on the three singing the last bars of a song.

Exuberant mood. Sound rather soft. Pom-pom-pom, like the Swingles.
PEG *carries the tune. The waltz that grinds out of merry-go-rounds: 'When you are in love, It's the loveliest night of the year . . .' The men do a unison dum-di-di bass. Slight shambles. Also triumph.*

PEG: Now I want to do the [*Sings: dum-di-di*] bass. Abberley do the tune.

MAX: It won't be any good that way. The two people doing the bass have got to be the same pitch.

PEG: Well, let's try. Abberley: [*Gives him a note*]. Max: [*Their note*].

    They do it. ABBERLEY *sings with his head down. Looking at the sheets. Concentrated.* PEG *has her head up and neck craned, like a dog baying at the moon.* MAX *does it efficiently and stolidly. Born pipe-smoker.* PEG *is married to* ABBERLEY.

ABBERLEY [*unusual excitement*]: Now me with her. It worked fine. We were beautiful.

MAX [*pleased*]: You mean I do the tune?

    Another go. Subdued rowdiness. Hot drinks out of thermoses.

MAX: What time is it?

ABBERLEY: Getting on for five in the morning.

PEG [*eager voice*]: Is it Friday?

ABBERLEY [*solicitous about her*]: No, we've barely embarked on Thursday yet.

    PEG *lies on elbow with her back to him, watching* MAX.

MAX: I think I'll relax for a while. We had a short night.

    MAX *puts on radio earphones and leans back with eyes closed. His spotlight snaps off. He remains faintly visible.*

PEG [*slight panic*]: Don't go to sleep: We were having fun. [ABBERLEY *looks at her back.*]

PEG: He's left us. He's quit. God damn him. Are we over? [*Dread in* ABBERLEY.]

ABBERLEY [*fierce*]: No. [*Sad.*] Are we?

PEG: Shall we both take a small pill and sleep it out until later?

[*Makes sturdy attempt to staunch the dread. Silence. She takes a pill anyway.*]

27

PEG [*without looking at Abberley*]: What could I do to cheer you up?

ABBERLEY: You're going to leave me, aren't you?
  [*Silence.*]

ABBERLEY: I know you want to, now.
  [*Silence.*]

ABBERLEY: Why?

PEG: It's not as good as it was. I remember when it was wonderful.
  [*Silence.*]

PEG: No, wrong ... I put that wrong. I don't mean that anything about us, about yourself and me, has fallen off. I mean longer ago than that. Much longer.

ABBERLEY: My dear love, you make yourself sound so old. I can't bear to hear you speak of yourself like that. You're very young.

PEG: I meant very long ago.

ABBERLEY: When you were with your *mother*? Good Christ. We must be better off together than that.

PEG: Don't be Freudian.

ABBERLEY: You're beautiful. Brush your hair.

PEG: Why?

ABBERLEY: I like watching it. Hell, why can't you do as you're told for me? You know that's what you're supposed to do. [*Continues to sit up and watch her for his own pleasure, rapt. Angry voice.*] Let me go to sleep.
  [*Pause.*]

ABBERLEY: You're still lying there keeping me awake. Are you going to drop off or not? There are some manners left, not to speak of anxiety. I've got to see you out, haven't I? [*Pause.*] Apart from that, who'd pass up the chance of an idle moment together? Without him? [*Pause.*] All the same, if you're just going to lie there keeping me awake, I've got to go to sleep. [*Grandeur.*] There's a man I should be defending in court all day and it's nearly dawn. [*Lies back.*] It's going to be dawn. You don't know what it's like, trying to go to sleep.
  [*Pause.*]

ABBERLEY [*hope*]: Are you awake?

PEG [*wide-awake voice*]: No.

ABBERLEY: Leave now, my darling, if you're going to, I beg of you. [*Pause.*] What's been the matter? I don't understand.

PEG: We've got too many things.

ABBERLEY: *What?*

PEG: I'm probably wrong. [*Pause. Soft voice.*] Somehow we landed up with too many things.

ABBERLEY [*shouts*]: I've got to go to sleep. [*Pause.*] How do you expect me to go to sleep after you've told me something like that? What am I to do? Something terrible's going to happen.

PEG: Thursdays are never easy. In fact they're bloody awful. Shall we have some sardines? A headline yesterday said: 'Saturday cancelled for lack of support.' [*Pause.*] I suppose it was a sporting event. A social event. Badminton. [*Excited.*] Gliding. Jam bottling. [*Pause.*] What a shame. *Saturday* unsupported. That's the best one.

ABBERLEY [*shouts*]: Shut up. I can't hear what you're thinking. [*Pause. Loud voice.*] I can hear you thinking something awful.

PEG: What could I do to stop you troubling?

ABBERLEY: Promise me not to – [*Pause.*] I could kill you for making me ask you that. One has no right.

PEG: Shall I come into your bed?

ABBERLEY: No room.

PEG: Are you all right?

ABBERLEY: That's my business.

[*He is gazing at his machine. So is she.*]

ABBERLEY: Get the sardines. Sardines would be nice. [*Pause.*] They wouldn't be forlorn, would they?

PEG [*firm voice*]: Eating in the night is never forlorn.

ABBERLEY: True. Then let's have caramels and you won't have to go away.

[PEG *starts to kick her sheets off.*]

ABBERLEY [*panic*]: Don't!

Penelope Gilliatt

PEG: You can't stop me.

[ABBERLEY *sighs, lies back, pulls the sheet up to his chin and pretends to sleep.* PEG *opens a drawer and gets out a nail file from a manicure set. The noise alerts* MAX. *Watches her. Anxiety. She gets out of bed and works on the screws pinning the legs to the floor. Her wires show. On all fours, she turns her machine around in* MAX'S *direction, and ours.* MAX *watches intently. Green track of pulse-beat bouncing like a ping pong ball.* ABBERLEY *talking over her as soon as she leaves bed.*]

ABBERLEY [*terror*]: You can't do that, you'll come unplugged, we can't do it, in our condition, not fair, we can't be expected. Now I can't see your set. Damn you, what if you've stopped, how'm I supposed? [*He gets out of bed himself. Stands with back to her with hands in pockets, looking at wall.*]

PEG [*all fours*]: Stop pretending there's a window.

ABBERLEY: I'm thinking.

PEG: No you're not, you're feeling, I can tell.

[PEG *tries to go over to* ABBERLEY. *Wires won't reach him. Stands at nearest point to him. Arms slightly forward.*]

PEG: I thought if I could push them together.

ABBERLEY: You're supposed to be someone I look after.
[*Silence.*]

ABBERLEY [*rage*]: Your energy, O.K., I know it's a miracle, yes. I'd be grateful for it if I were dead. I know it's the best thing that ever happened to me.

PEG: Well?

ABBERLEY: But I can't deal with it. Dear God. [*Pause.*] Rest His soul. [*Pause. Turns around, sees her machine now facing her bed again and in his view. Watches. Relief, then boredom.* MAX'S *eyes not removed from it.* ABBERLEY *leans against his bedhead. Tries radio earphones.*]

ABBERLEY: They're talking about *food* on the *music* programme. 'Non-caloric ...' [*Disgust. Attention.*] 'Flaming kebab tonight on our Excalibur's sword.' [*Takes off earphones.*] Putting out announcements like that before *breakfast.* [*Lofty.*] What's going on out there? [*Gets back*

into bed.] Excalibur. Show-off. I can't stand pushy food.
I like your food.
　[*Pause. Watches her, again on her hands and knees. Urgent
voice.*]
ABBERLEY: I'm hungry. [*Pause.*] Girls shouldn't do things
like that.
PEG: Well, you help, then.
ABBERLEY [*seigneurish*]: I'll get a carpenter tomorrow.
PEG [*contemptuous voice*]: Tomorrow!
ABBERLEY: What's tomorrow done?
PEG: What guarantee?
ABBERLEY: Darling, tomorrow comes over the hill in
hordes, like the Chinese.
PEG: *You* believe that? Old black-heart? [*Sits back on heels.*]
What a good day.
ABBERLEY: I was only trying out the idea. [*Pause.*] I seem
to believe it as long as you're still ticking over nicely.
　[PEG *goes back to work. Men's gazes on her machine.*]
ABBERLEY [*rage*]: Why won't you ever do what I say?
That bed is pinned to the floor for a purpose.
PEG: Don't be religious. [*Pause.* ABBERLEY *looks for some-
thing by his bed.*] What are you doing now?
ABBERLEY: My pen's gone. [*He shines his torch at her bed-
side table.*] You've got my ballpoint pen.
PEG: I didn't know it was yours. No ballpoint can be *your*
ballpoint. Ballpoints are *people's*.
　[PEG *sits on the edge of her bed.* ABBERLEY *knows it
without looking.*]
ABBERLEY: Now what is it?
PEG: Darling, go to sleep.
ABBERLEY: How can I when you're wanting to move the
bed and I don't want you to? I've given you all this.
We've got all this. It isn't enough for you, and I hate you
for it, and I want you to go before you decide to leave me,
and I love you, and how am I expected to stand being
cooped up with him.
PEG: Yes.
ABBERLEY: Yes what?

PEG: That's what it's like.

ABBERLEY [*rage*]: You're too young to decide that. You're mine. [*Shouts.*] Where am I to live?

PEG: We've no choice.

ABBERLEY: You're where I live.

PEG: I'm here.

ABBERLEY: You're mine.

PEG: Things have changed.
    [*Silence.*]

ABBERLEY: You've no business. You're too young.

PEG: I feel as old as the hills.

ABBERLEY [*weeps*]: I decide.
    [*Silence.*]

ABBERLEY: Could we have your lamp off? It's too bright. You will use 150 watt bulbs. [*Hatred of beautiful room.*] It's like living in a bleeding watch factory. [*Looks at* MAX]. Of course, there are times when he's company. As technologists go.

PEG [*attentive voice*]: Do you think your eyes need seeing to?

ABBERLEY: You can't do this.

PEG: I'm in love with him.

    [ABBERLEY *whips head away. Pause.*]

ABBERLEY: I'll kill you.

PEG: I could go to a hotel for a bit.

ABBERLEY: Perhaps you won't have to go far.
    [*Lights snap off. Lights snap on. Nothing displaced. Much time passed. People look the same.* ABBERLEY *talking cheerfully to* MAX. PEG *now* MAX's *wife. Her spotlight off.*

ABBERLEY: A lot to be said for it. No more upset nights. A man needs time to hide himself. Where is she?

PEG [*voice from semi-dark*]: I'm here.

ABBERLEY [*to* MAX]: How is she?

MAX: Fine.

ABBERLEY: I wanted to remind her about her driving licence. It's expired and she never remembers.

MAX [*impatient*]: You can always find us, God knows.

ABBERLEY [*chatty*]: She came back for her books. She took a painting someone gave us as a wedding present. I'll have to get the wall repainted. The place is a wreck. [*Hand gesture at serene emptiness. No change, ever.*]

MAX: But she told me she didn't take a thing?

ABBERLEY [*impatient voice*]: The paint's a completely different colour underneath. Nasty patch. I'll never get anything the same shape. I'm supposed to be a lawyer. I haven't got time to go traipsing around art galleries. Where is she?

MAX: She should be at the dentist's all day tomorrow.

ABBERLEY: Her teeth are perfect.

MAX: She has four impacted wisdom teeth.

ABBERLEY: No decay?

MAX: I'll ask her, if you like. It's not the usual thing we spend time discussing.

ABBERLEY [*addressing himself to his electrocardiograph, loud voice*]: *Scientists are pompous asses.* [*To* MAX, *shouting immediately.*] As if you hadn't both got all the time in the world. [*Polite voice.*] Could we all meet and talk some day?

MAX: What the hell else do we do?

ABBERLEY: I meant, meet formally. It might make the difference? [*Pause.*] I want to give her a Christmas present. I thought it would go with her hair. As long as you don't mind. A cowhide rug. For you both, really.

MAX [*startled*]: Then what colour is cow?

ABBERLEY: Have you forgotten. *All* cows are *brown.*

MAX: *Some* are black and white. [*Pompously.*] Brown – scarcely – can scarcely be said to match fair hair.

ABBERLEY: *Fair?* Her hair was always brown. Quite a dark brown.

MAX: It's touched up. Tinted. What we used to call dyed. Longer ago, what we used to call helped.

ABBERLEY: She never dyed her hair when she was living with me.

MAX: It's gone grey. You haven't noticed. Peroxiding it seemed a hopeful idea. She did it after she'd been ill.

ABBERLEY [*rage*]: Nothing is ever wrong with her. She's as

strong as a horse. Nothing was ever wrong with her in our day. She was going to outlive everyone.

[*Pause.*]

MAX [*helping*]: Fine woman.

ABBERLEY [*gritty*]: Girl.

[*Max humours him and reads a book.*]

ABBERLEY: I suppose I should get somewhere to live. I really do need a place. This [*hatred*] well-bred – nothing.

MAX: It isn't bad, though.

ABBERLEY: No. [*Pause.*] Nice of you.

MAX: Excuse me for asking, but what did you chat about when you were alone? I don't find chatting very easy. [*Pause.*] You've noticed.

ABBERLEY: You're necessary. It seems. [*Gracious.*] No reflection on you. [*He gets out his torch.*] Do you mind?

MAX: Please.

[ABBERLEY *goes over towards* PEG's *bed, trailing his wires. Studies her face in torchlight. Returns to his own bed.*]

MAX: O.K.?

ABBERLEY: Exactly the same.

[*Pause.*]

MAX: Do we really have to go through this nightly ritual?

ABBERLEY: It's not the easiest hour.

MAX: Do you find science fiction helpful?

ABBERLEY: Sodium amytal.

MAX: Could I have some?

[ABBERLEY *throws the bottle. They take a pill each.*]

MAX: Cheers. Down the hatch.

ABBERLEY: Life has its rewards.

MAX: What did you talk about? In the old days?

ABBERLEY: Hard to say. [*Pause.*] We just *talked*. Sometimes we spoke our minds, sometimes not. What are you asking? You could have heard it all, if you'd had the ears. We had quite a lot of laughs. She played the mouth organ. She liked that. I gave her a ridiculously expensive mouth organ one Christmas, much like a cocktail cabinet. Et cetera, et cetera. I know her very well. We never ran out of things to say. Is that what you mean? [*Glee.*] Are you in a blue funk about running out of things to say?

MAX: What *sort* of things did you talk about?

ABBERLEY: Well. [*Pause. Haughty.*] Heavens, man. [*Pause.*] There was food, for instance. [*Pause.*] And her childhood, for another thing. She had a foul father. We had many a cheerful chat about that. He used to swing her by the leg to fortify her character.

MAX [*shakes head. Earnest*]: Those methods never work.

ABBERLEY: And I suppose you could say it was.

MAX: What?

ABBERLEY: Fortified.

MAX [*upper hand*]: *What?* She's as weak as a kitten. I've never heard her argue back in her life. Can't you hear her teeth chattering in the night?

ABBERLEY [*not listening, smoking*]: Yes, she's a salty fighter. There's one who knows how to whip up trouble and find out where you stand. That's the thing. Spine. You can rely on her for that.

MAX: Stop using the present tense.

ABBERLEY [*patient*]: Look, we still live together, don't we? We're still stuck in this place. [*Cordial.*] Couldn't you murder it? If you weren't here, Peg and I could have beaten it.

MAX: My dear Abberley.

ABBERLEY: Don't you my-dear-Abberley me. You're a technological grease-swabber.

MAX: You don't know a thing about her any longer. I don't believe you ever did. She's a mouse. She's also getting long in the tooth and she's subject to migraine.

[ABBERLEY *puts his hand to his head for a second.*]

ABBERLEY: I'm the better judge. We were married for the formative period.

MAX: She always told me you didn't believe in Freud.

ABBERLEY: No, it was *her* that didn't. [*Pause.*] Is that right? It's all screwed up.

MAX: She forgets too.

ABBERLEY: Oh, *no.* Her memory is impeccable. Except for dates.

MAX: Not now. [*Kind.*] She's changed, you see. It only proves my point.

[*Lights snap on. Lights snap up.* PEG *still in semi-dark. Some other dawn.*]

ABBERLEY: Where is she now? Max? Where now?

MAX: She's supposed to go into the hospital.

ABBERLEY: Save us, what for?

MAX: Just a check-up.

ABBERLEY: When I left her – no, say, say, to put it another way, why not be kind, second husband, after all, when she left me for you, when she quit, she left in perfect repair.

MAX: Well, she's fallen into rack and ruin now.

ABBERLEY: You can't have looked after her. [*Frantic.*] You'll be telling me she's got arthritis next.

MAX: Rheumatism, a bit.

ABBERLEY: Oh no, oh no. [*Pause.*] It's not right.

MAX: I never understand what you liked about her. She always says she irritated you. She says she behaved like hell to you.

ABBERLEY [*withdrawn*]: It isn't like that at all.

MAX: Wasn't.

ABBERLEY: All right. I probably didn't pay enough heed. At the time. That's crossed my mind.

[ABBERLEY *gets out of bed, trailing wires, and looks at her cardiograph. Sits on the floor for a bit, watching it. Tries to get near her, but the wires won't let him closer than the bedside table. He looks at her pills.*]

ABBERLEY: She's got plenty of phenobarbital. We won't run out. [*Pause. Rage as he tries again to reach her.*] Rheumatism!

MAX: It's to be expected.

ABBERLEY [*shouts*]: No. [*Soft voice.*] You can't be looking after her. Everything about her has always worked.

MAX: You talk about her like a landlord.

[ABBERLEY *turns his back and goes to his bed.*]

MAX: Temper about the roof falling in. Woodworm. Dry rot. Maintenance. Power failure. Fuses. Normal wear and tear. To be expected, to be expected. [ABBERLEY *can't stand it.*]

ABBERLEY: *You've let it happen.* You've let her wear out. [*Pause.*]

ABBERLEY: She's beautiful. You should look at her. Young.

MAX: I *live* with her. She's showing the normal signs of middle age. You don't grasp. People deteriorate.

ABBERLEY [*snorting*]: Peg?

MAX: I call her Margaret.

ABBERLEY: Good god. [*Pause.*] Does she answer to it? [MAX *gets up and sits on the edge of his bed and smokes a pipe. Pause.*]

MAX: Do you think we should be making more of an effort, or is this as good as one can manage? Considering what's against us?

ABBERLEY: We might listen to the radio for a time. Both of us. [*Silence for a short while.* ABBERLEY *alone listens to his radio earphones.* MAX *sits thinking.* ABBERLEY *takes off earphones.*]

ABBERLEY: It's nice to be able to talk, isn't it? [MAX *walks over towards* PEG *and looks at her. It means unplugging his wires from his body. Done casually. That sort of man. He kisses her.* ABBERLEY *watches, he nods. Gets anxious about* MAX.]

ABBERLEY: Would you mind turning your cardiograph around a little so that I can see it? [MAX *swivels set. Dead screen visible to us.* ABBERLEY *watches.* MAX *plugs himself in again. Normal graph.* ABBERLEY *relieved.*]

ABBERLEY: How's sex, if I may ask?

MAX: Fine.

ABBERLEY: Good. [*Pause.*] I – she must have said this to you.

MAX: She doesn't talk unpleasantly about you. Or give anything away. Is *that* what you thought? [*Pause.*] If so, I'll wake her up. I won't be party to you bitching yourself on the sly. You can do it with her as a witness, so there.

[MAX *holds still.*]

ABBERLEY: Hush. I'm a difficult man. Naggy. I could
never stand the worry of her taking her wires off. [*Pause.
Recollection of that terror.*] So you might say sex was a bit
thin in this two thirds of the room.

MAX: That's anxiety. [*Patronage.*]

ABBERLEY: I'm furious with you about her teeth. What
have you been doing to her? Any operations you haven't
told me about? [*Acidity, over great fear.*]

[PEG *wakes up. Her spotlight snaps on. Cheery mood.*]

PEG: Hello, my loves. Oh Christ, it's Sunday. Shall we have
an aspirin at once? We'll need a bit of cheering up.

ABBERLEY [*to* MAX, *serious, after scrutiny of* PEG]: She's
exactly the same.

PEG: No.

ABBERLEY [*hiding face*]: You mean there's sign of toll.

MAX: Of what?

ABBERLEY: Toll.

[*Pause.*]

ABBERLEY: How dare she suffer? You're lying again. I
remember her. There wasn't a cloud. She was the sun-
niest girl I ever knew. Even in the mornings, heaven help
me, when burbling isn't exactly welcome. [*Pause.*] Pri-
marily, she belonged to me. Therefore, ultimately.
[*Pause.*] She *cannot* have changed.

PEG [*robust*]: I'm long in the tooth and short in the breath.
How about a drink before dawn breaks? [*Moved.*] Nice
to be together, isn't it? [*To* ABBERLEY, *making herself.*]
Darling, I have changed. You won't like my hair, for a
start. I've got thin. I'm not what I was.

ABBERLEY [*shouting*]: You're exactly the same. You haven't
changed. *He*'s let you go, if there's any question of it.

PEG: What month is it? October?

ABBERLEY [*to* MAX, *quick pick-up*]: There, see what I mean?
I know her backwards. See why I had to remind her
about the driving licence? Does she keep the insurance
premiums up? On her jewellery? I didn't give her enough.
Nothing much. But she wouldn't like it to be gone.

[PEG *is playing patience on her lap. Smile at* ABBERLEY. *We can see some bits of jewellery in her night-table drawer. She is wearing some beads now, hidden for the moment under her clothes.*]

MAX: It's November. It'll be her birthday before we can turn around. Feel free to give her anything you like. We don't go in for presents.

[PEG *smiles again at* ABBERLEY.]

PEG [*looking from one to another. Speaking brightly to close the gaps, as if at a party*]: So it's getting near Christmas. Is Christmas worse because of the activity, do you think, or because of God? It *can't* be the activity, can it? [*Pause.*] What are the lucky creeps doing out there? [*Pause.*] The thing that makes me believe in God is that there's a special kind of weather on Sundays. Only on Sundays. Muggy. Gives you a headache. There must be a God.

MAX: That's mood, my love, not weather, and the mood's because the shops are closed. [*Sucks pipe.*]

PEG: That's a housewifeish thing to say.

[PEG *makes a noise at herself (brr, shaking head). Packs up the patience and goes toward* MAX's *bed.*]

PEG: I expect I woke up at the wrong time. It'll be all right.

[MAX *gets up and takes off her hood. Long blonde hair falls out. She plaits it. Her beads show.*]

MAX: Who gave you those beads?

PEG: They're the ones I always wear.

[ABBERLEY *has looked away from her hair. Sad. But pleased about the beads. She sits on the bed and watches him.*]

PEG: Are you all right?

ABBERLEY: Fine.

PEG: How's Ronnie?

ABBERLEY: Fine.

PEG: How's George?

ABBERLEY: Fine.

PEG: How're Joe and Lil?

ABBERLEY: Fine.

PEG: Is Bob fine?

ABBERLEY: Fine.

PEG: Who else is fine?

ABBERLEY: Most of us. [*Pause.*] What have they done to your teeth and your bones? What are these migraines?

PEG: Thy wife, goat or mansion.

ABBERLEY: What?

PEG: Nothing.

ABBERLEY: You sound tired.

MAX: She isn't tired.

ABBERLEY: Stop translating for her. *We lived together*. We had a *life*.

PEG: You don't know me any more. You won't look. You do too much remembering.

ABBERLEY: I don't remember a thing about you. I don't remember the clothes you wore, or your beautiful hair, or the sardines, or the mouth organ. I recall nothing. I haven't owned you for ten years. Sixteen?

PEG [*to* MAX]: Stop him.

ABBERLEY: I gave up the title to you.

PEG: Max, help.

ABBERLEY: Dyeing your hair. Which side of the bed do you sleep on now? [*To* PEG.]

MAX: I sleep on the right hand side of my particular bed. When we share it. The right, seen from the head end.

ABBERLEY: So she's on the left. You've tried to change everything about her. She was on the track, don't you see? I don't believe she's better off. I have an idea of her. You're trying to take it away with all these dentists and bone-men and switching her side in bed. Does she still drink tea all the time?

MAX: Yes.

ABBERLEY [*to* PEG]: I told you you should take the Georgian teapot.

PEG [*tender voice*]: I told you I couldn't be cumbered. [*Pause.*] How is it?

ABBERLEY: What?

PEG: Our teapot.

　　[PEG *and* MAX *now begin to speak to each other.* ABBER-

LEY *takes off his watch and looks at it. Notes time carefully. Puts watch on table and records the time on a pad.*]

MAX [*to* PEG]: If we weren't having a civilized drink together I'd bash you for that '*our teapot*'.

[PEG *hums.*]

PEG: These are the middle years.

ABBERLEY: In a part of Greece, a remote part, a man who kills another man immediately takes over the dead man's wife. The care of her. The property. The sexual rights.

MAX [*to* PEG]: Make him shut up. What about all humming again?

ABBERLEY [*pursuing his own pointed anthropology and wanly fostering academicism*]: It's an intelligent union of heroics and economics. From the point of view of the man left alive.

PEG [*to* MAX]: Dear, you can see he is making an effort. Should we have a game?

[MAX *attends to the eternal pipe. Silence.*]

ABBERLEY [*to* PEG, *accusing, grieved*]: You've got other aches by now, I suppose.

PEG: I'm falling apart. The whole fabric. I need a relief fund. [*To* MAX] Why don't you draw something?

ABBERLEY: I'd better leave you together. Not that one can move. [*To* PEG] You're no further off than you were, I suppose.

PEG [*pause*]: The way I might have cared for you ... The people I could have done things for ... The place used to be lousy with them. Shall we have a drink? I don't feel very well.

ABBERLEY: You've let her rot away.

PEG [*to* ABBERLEY]: Are you frightened of dying at the moment?

ABBERLEY: Of you being ill. [*Looks at* MAX, *covertly.*] Shh. Not now.

PEG [*to* MAX]: I'm sorry. [MAX *shakes head. Smiles.*]

ABBERLEY: We're not doing badly. We're having a drink. [*Pause.*] My dear, the time we had – it wasn't what we meant. Some. Not enough of it.

PEG: No. [*Pause.*]

[ABBERLEY *looks at his own cardiograph for a time. Then turns it to audience, away from himself,* MAX, PEG. *Gets back into bed and looks at* MAX'S *machine instead.* PEG *speaks to air in outrage.*]

PEG: I can't see it. He must know I worry if I can't see it. How dare he not know that?

MAX: Oh dear, now you're going to get upset.

ABBERLEY: Don't get upset. Would you like one of my pills?

PEG: I'm *not* upset. Yes, I would [*to* ABBERLEY]. Are you all right?

ABBERLEY: Fine. [*Throws pills to her.*] Would you like my solitaire board? I've got too many things. My eyes hurt. I've got earache. I wish it would buck up and be Monday. Lousy dump. [*Pause.*] Perhaps I could yet do better. Scrap the thing so far and begin another. Something I could bring to a decent conclusion. One gripes and holds off and bangs the pillows and thinks the real thing is to come and then one starts to lose the thread. My dear friends, this is it, yes? This. I realized that at a particularly good moment, at 5.48 this morning. I took account of the time. Something pleasant happened. . . . Peg, I've grown immensely fat. You may not notice it under the sheets. Clean sheets a great comfort, eh? [*Laughs.*]

PEG: Getting old has its funny side, I grant you that.

ABBERLEY: Would you do me the goodness of turning your electrocardiograph around to me? In honour of our – past. Away from him. Until it's light.

[PEG *turns it round to him, crawling to bottom of bed.*]

ABBERLEY: Can we switch the lamps off?

[*Spotlights snap off. Pale light through scrim wall.* MAX *reads by torchlight under the sheets.* PEG *crawls back to do the same.*]

ABBERLEY: You still have a very nice rump. The rump is often the first to fail.

[*We see the three cardiographs recording.* ABBERLEY'S *faces us. The other two machines face him, diagonally visible to us;* ABBERLEY *watches them.*]

ABBERLEY: Thank you.

Penelope Gilliatt

The Last to Go

'Get out,' said Stephen Brandt's best friend. 'And shut up.'

'I am out,' Stephen said, not moving from his best friend's own armchair in Dulwich. 'To all intents and purposes. And I'm effectively shut up because I've been kicked out of my job and also because you don't seem to have heard a word I've been saying.' He tried to leave the chair and go, but didn't badly enough want to, and carried on with a furious daydream of what the trades-union movement might come to represent in England, although England was only half his country.

The best friend, Felix – an affectionate, forgetful, hypomanic man, passionately expert in animal physiology and the history of Communism – yelled benignly at his wife for more coffee and said again, 'Get out. You're boring when you're like this. Go and talk to somebody from the library.'

'There is no more library. I've been sacked.'

'"Jesus wept."'

'What?'

'It's the shortest verse in the Bible.'

'I know that. There is no more Bible.'

'You're really down, aren't you?' said Felix's wife, who had come in with a jar of instant coffee and a jug of water no more than fairly hot, which increased Stephen's worry that many things were falling behind. He had memories of Vienna before the 1939 war, and liked people who took care over such things as coffee – proper, expensive coffee – as he tried to himself, however much he decided to ignore most of the facts of being poor.

'Not altogether down,' he said.

'He's just caught Socialism,' said Felix.

'All over again,' Stephen said. 'I didn't think you could get it a second time. I can't imagine why, when the Labour Party's such a swindle. It must have been Czechoslovakia. That possibility.'

'Probably chemical,' Felix said. 'I've known of chemical conversions to ideology.'

'It's more like love,' Stephen said seriously. 'You never think you can get that twice.'

Felix pondered a bad time that Stephen had had with a girl a while ago, and fiddled with his shortwave radio. It was believed by the other people in his street, the owners of the other semi-detached red brick villas with Victorian stained glass over the front doors and children's tricycles in the halls, that Felix was a Communist spy. His absorption with Mao and Castro was so open that the neighbours took it for a double bluff, and each new discovery of an agent transmitting messages from some ordinary-looking English suburb increased the tension of their interest in the land-mine which was surely bound one day to go off in their own street. Stephen knew of the rumour and had neither evidence nor time for it. He had been Felix's friend since 1938. They were young Communists together after Stephen fled Austria. His father, now dead, had been an English book translator living in Vienna. His mother, also dead, was really German, but she had called herself Austrian in an impulse of cowardice that Stephen rather cherished her for. The times had made him mistrust the militant kinds of heroism, though he unjustly saw himself as deficient in fortitude of another sort. He had been born with a curved spine and stood five feet.

'What are you going to live on?' said Felix's wife.

'I don't need much.'

'And what are you going to do?'

'I'm going to resign from the Labour Party to make my position clear, and then I don't know.'

Even Felix refrained from asking him who would notice.

Felix's wife started talking about poetry, which she wrote, while Felix shouted about his last visit to Castro. Stephen listened carefully to both, his head forward and down, like a horse's hanging over a gate, which was a way he had and not altogether due to the curve in his spine.

'I thought I might go to America and help the anti-draft students around the Army camps,' he said.

Felix's wife began to recite her poetry, and wondered about his air fare, and gave him some coffee. Felix thought of Czechoslovakia and then careered into a fantasy of Ho Chi Minh gossiping about the minor members of the English Royal Family. He started to shout again.

'Though perhaps one should try to do something to rescue Socialism here,' Stephen said softly, through both of them. 'I thought I might go and talk in factories.'

'You're out of your mind!' Felix yelled. 'England's as dead as a doornail. Greedy. Dozy. Worse than America. The whole system has to be changed.'

'Sh-h-h,' said Felix's wife.

'Why?' said Felix.

'There's a nice worried American on the run from the draft next door.'

'Well, I said we were even worse, didn't I?' Felix glared at her.

'Then why do you like it here?' Stephen said. 'You love England as much as anyone I know.'

'It's the only possible place to live,' Felix said, putting on a record of North Vietnamese songs with the volume up very loud.

Stephen made a few moderate reservations about England in his own soft voice, which was audible over the hub-bub like some supersonic protest. Felix's wife went on stoutly reading her poetry as if she were not shy, roaring to keep the beat against the Vietnamese and walking round and round the dining table in time with herself.

'What *do* you like about England?' Stephen said again.

'It's *mellow*, Stephen!' Felix bawled angrily, on his feet, with his arms swinging on a curve away from his body and looking abnormally long. 'MELLOW!' he shouted, louder still. Stephen laughed, and Felix felt vaguely resentful, but it was fine to see his friend laughing at the moment, even at his expense, so he brushed the mood away and continued with an invention about Mao studying Princess Anne's record on gymkhanas. He appeared to be airborne, but he was watching Stephen out of the corner of his eye.

'I'm going home,' Stephen said, and no one asked where that was. He had just been booted out of his digs, for the nth time, because the landlady had complained about the noise of a child who had stayed with him on the way home for half-term. But presumably he had a place to go, and he would prefer to keep that problem to himself.

'He looks minute,' Felix's wife said, watching him from their gate as he marched down the road to the bus stop.

'He could never stand up and lecture for weeks on end in all those factories.' Felix remembered the gang of them at the beginning of the world war, with Stephen, stomping around reviling the call-up, deciding on conscientious objection for himself, shaking off the hand of any acquaintance who tried to help him speed over a dangerous crossing, and talking about the anti-militarist statement he would make to the court. None of his friends could possibly have pointed out that there was no question of his ever passing the physical.

'Men are very fragile,' Felix's wife said, looking at her giant husband, who was standing under a street lamp stirring his arms like propellers.

'I'm going for a walk, dear,' he said, absently. He always went for a walk about this hour. And then he got up again at half past five to read.

'I wish we needed the same number of hours' sleep,' she said. 'I wish we went to bed at the same time. I always fall off while I'm waiting for you.'

'I liked the coffee tonight,' he said, not allowing that it

was the same instant coffee as ever, and to deserve the goodness she determined to go up to Soho tomorrow for some fresh espresso beans.

Then she swore out of the blue and said, 'The truth is, you know, I suddenly hope Stephen doesn't come again. Not unless he's more manageable. He's upsetting. I hate just anyone dropping in. I can't stand it.'

'He's not just anyone. He's Stephen.'

'Those terrifying high hopes. What's he going to do with them? Did his back look worse to you?'

As happened in their life together, Felix was humbled for a flash by a sense that she had caught something he had missed: something wild in the air that Stephen had brought with him. 'Come on, old girl,' he shouted, 'calm down!' and later he found her a scientific paper to read, which she liked.

'Here,' said Stephen Brandt to life, walking down the Strand at eleven o'clock the next dampish morning and moving his lips without a sound. 'You think I've had enough. Well, I haven't, not by a long chalk, and I'm not the tramp I look, either. It's a bad time, admitted, there's truth in that, but I shouldn't choose to be out of it. A lax and, O.K., a dishonourable time. Immigration Act, Rhodesia, Gomulka, Prague, America having a national nervous breakdown, the soul of England on the ropy side. Hope in the students, as long as you don't get too utopian about it nor start to laugh. Expect nothing. That's the trick. Conceive of the boundless, but expect nothing whatever. There won't be an apocalypse from English students, not from that quarter, I shouldn't suppose. Though who can tell? Stupidity of trying to conclude. In the sense of reaching any conclusions. Also, of course, in the sense of ending. I have never been further from suicide in my life, though I imagine my friends would find it quite opportune. Understandably. My lack of means is extreme, granted, and I look bad, skin white, mouth chapped, body apparently even shorter than usual, eye roaming and I daresay a bit fretful, trousers in bad shape, attention astray for a book lying around to pinch or even an old magazine, since I sold a few volumes I should now like to have kept, in exchange for a slug of what turned out to be the world's nastiest though cheapest whisky. A poor impulse. I ordered a quadruple. Something I've never done before or since in my life. It was very necessary, and it made a sunny improvement in the event. So one looks forward.'

'Listen,' Stephen said to a woman at Labour Party head-quarters in Transport House. 'I've come to resign.'

After a pause, while she knitted and changed to a new ball of wool, she surprisingly said, 'Oh dear.'

'That's nice of you,' he said, blood having started to boil.

'No call to be formal about it,' she said. 'If you feel like resigning, all you have to do is let your dues lapse. I don't suppose they're paid up anyway. They never are.'

'Mine are.'

'Don't you be so sure. Bertrand Russell's weren't and a nice pickle he got himself into, though I'd put it all down to that secretary if I were asked. Speaking personally.'

'Anyway, I want to hand in my card. I want my position to be clear. I've written a letter to my Member of Parliament, but I want it to be clear at headquarters.'

'What?'

'That Socialism in England has turned out to be a bitter farce.' He looked at her knitting, which continued, approaching the heel of the sock in progress, and wondered if she was ever going to glance at his card on the counter.

'And who am I supposed to send it to, may I ask?' She banged down her knitting. 'I can't read the signature.' With distaste: 'You're not famous or something, are you?'

'No.'

'I can't do anything with the matter if you won't give me the details. No skin off my nose.'

He stayed silent. Chin not more than four inches above the sill of her cubicle. She stood to get a pencil. Five feet seven, eight.

'Stephen Brandt, is it?' she said. 'It seems to be paid up.'

'Since 1940.'

'It's a meaningless gesture, you know. Handing it in.' She spoke coldly, and he hated her, and the height of her, and of a man behind her. The tall, those engrossers of manhood, those hyperbolic exemplifiers of the species, the monsters who overlook us.

'There's no such thing as a meaningless gesture,' he said, after emptying himself of that thought. 'If it *is* a gesture, then it must always have a meaning.'

'Well.' She sniffed, and considered. 'There's an interesting idea,' she said, throwing him into next week with the surprise of it. People change, he told himself. I might remember not to treat people as if they could only act in one way. I suppose they could always act differently.

'Are you turning Tory? That's all they're going to want to know,' she said.

'No.' He thought. Is that really all they'll want to know? And proceeded to plan a call on some of his old Communist Party mates during his walk back home.

'It's odd that I haven't heard of you. You're sure you're not a celebrity masquerading?' She looked at his clothes with disbelief and a little pity. 'Otherwise I don't know why you've come. I mean, you're not a nut.'

'No?'

'We've experience in recognizing nuts in this place.'

Well, he thought, she said I'm not a nut. One can reckon that to be all to the good, from a stranger. To be plain, I'm a bit exhausted, secretly, about the intellectual advantages that are supposed (by intellectuals) to accrue from being physically underendowed or peculiar-looking, though it's possible to keep up the front in public and many a gulled beloved has supposed that this joke of a frame is where my energy comes from. (*What energy?*) Hellfire to, for instance, Annabel, for her loving farewell about 'understanding the beleaguered ferocity of the uncommon'. Silly bird. Too much upbringing can mess a person about. She meant she was frightened, didn't she? She said I was too much for her, and I assume she thought she was being admiring, though she certainly meant I was not enough. Boiling oil on the head of her. Where is she now? On the right side, of course, doing her best about Vietnam, et cetera. And not betraying the past, either, not rewriting our private history to suit herself. That isn't her flaw at all. She said she wanted to go to Peking. With her children. Ye gods, I said, with the babies? There are crèches in China, she said. Well, yes, I know that, O.K., I said, you're their mother, and you decided against their father for reasons I take to be desolate, but wouldn't some Asian studies in St James's Square at the Institute of International Affairs be less perilous until they are both over, say, four? And then she quite confounded me by doing exactly what I advised, and I'd always thought she took me for a crank whose horse sense, if any, was a forced calm not to be heeded. And when the babies were both a ripe four-plus, and she did indeed go off to Peking and left them with me, the ensuing fun made me wonder sometimes whether I was their father, which is no question to put, since the answer should be proffered, I suppose. I should like to have been a parent, a real English Socialist, a stunning diver on the side, and a foppish dresser. Just look at these clothes. I wish I were an orator. Or a political writer of great eloquence. I should like to speak to people of their other lives.

Then Brandt went into a tea shop, in spite of feeling that his new landlady's fried bread for breakfast was going to be more than enough to see him through the day. Food lay like clods of clay in his stomach and it rained, but he was supported by a sense of majesty in ideas and even in himself for having them, though this latter maintenance came and went. He thought of a Socialist future for his half-country, and conceived the hope of a job in which he might have the luck to be gripped by some stupendous ire of work, trying to avoid the spectacle of the people around him and in the wet street outside, which pointed out a fraternal indifference in the world that was the last perception he cared to harbour. It was a time when he was immensely drawn to panache, and he felt done with the prim and the hangdog for good. He suddenly saw Annabel passing in the street outside. It was a year or more since they had met, but he ran out of the shop and clung to her elbow. They ran ill-assortedly up the street in the drizzle. She was the taller and also he ran with difficulty, but she was used to the coupling and minded nothing. They talked as they ran, and he was elated. They made plans to spend the day together. He experienced a considerable longing for a whole life of shambles and baked beans.

They started for a Communist Party hangout. He warned her, and himself, that the call was likely to be a waste of spirit. All the same, he dearly hoped that the mood there might match his own. He felt like the man in an old music-hall joke who hammers on the dentist's door with a wet sponge, the need to get in conflicting powerfully with the longing to flee.

As it turned out, of course, the people in the seedy upstairs room couldn't provide any of the raw exuberance he wanted. At the same time, he was much too committed to them by years in common for their limp urbanity to strike him as funny in world-changers. What they expressed was not so much any possibility of revolution as a sort of chivalrous exasperation at things as they would always be. He introduced Annabel and told the watchful, exhausted-looking ring of people that she was working at night with a set of young Left-wingers who published a broadsheet the old guard knew all too well. It was immediately clear that he had put his foot in it. While an angry woman in a cardigan sadly toasted herself a crumpet by the jet of a gas fire, he tried to shift to another topic. He said he was thinking of going to America for a while. He also said, rashly, that he felt stirred by the efforts of American radicals. This turned out to be essentially the same menacing subject as the earlier one.

'Riot guides and drug protests and minor jokes about policemen,' said a man in a mackintosh, standing up by the gas fire and talking fixedly about the broadsheet, eyeing it in its filing place. 'They don't know the power of what they're up against. They won't define it. They pinch most of what they say from the student press in America and throw in a few tags from Colonel Ojukwu. Never enough to be serious. That's the thing; they're simply not very substantial.'

'They suggested putting marbles under the hoofs of police horses,' said the woman with the crumpet.

'She's not being sentimental,' the man in the mackintosh said. '*Any* measures would be permissible if there were a structure of thought behind them.'

'They don't know any history,' the woman said. 'They don't even know anything about the war. I sometimes think they have a neurosis about not having been in the blitz.'

Feeling hampered, Stephen managed to plough on with a story about a Yale graduate who was in prison for fighting the Vietnam draft.

'There's no weight to isolated acts of self-aggrandizing heroism in a decaying society,' said a man who was generally nice, and who bore on his forehead the triangular scar of a marble paperweight that had been thrown at him by his best friend, a Tory, for a sentence like that.

'Self-aggrandizing?' said Stephen, rising to the bait when he knew better. 'He's in prison.'

'Well, he's celebrity-seeking enough to have made you talk about him.'

'Scarcely anyone has heard his *name*. You hadn't. I asked him once why I'd never seen him mentioned in any of the endless stuff about his movement, and he said he thought some of them had to stay anonymous. "Look at the famous ones," he said. "They can't move. They're pinned. We have to have spokesmen, but we also have to leave some of us free to do things," he said.'

'What's special about that?' asked the woman by the gas fire.

'I just thought it was rather remarkable in a boy of twenty-three. It seemed grown-up,' said Stephen.

'It's all by the way,' said a thin man impatiently from behind his desk, which was stacked with political magazines. There was a photograph in the chaos. His wife in their garden. He had a collection of little ivory animals on his pencil tray. He arranged them in a Noah row as he talked. Stephen found it impossible not to be fond of him. 'There's no programme,' the man said frantically, putting a bear behind a hippopotamus. 'It's the vice of America to believe in the random.'

'No, I don't think so,' Annabel said suddenly, and then stopped.

'Go on,' Stephen said to her.

'It's only that I think, maybe, that it's more the vice of America – no, not vice, I don't think, but difficulty – to be moralistic in politics. Is that right?'

The man behind the desk paused and said, 'It's a point,' with no interest at all.

Annabel dried up entirely.

'Haven't a clue what that signifies,' said the woman by the fire, speaking through the crumpet. 'Would anyone like the other half of my crumpet? Speak up or I'll have wolfed it.'

'Have you got a boy friend working with that lot?' the scarred man asked Annabel with a pounce.

'No,' Stephen said, stabbed, just realizing that she had. He stood up and walked to the window of the cold, cold room, putting aside with contempt his lifelong habit of arranging to be seated so as to hide his size when he was about to say anything that interested him. 'The trait she's talking about. It's a confusion. It gives a moral force that's spurious ... that's troubling to America ... a moral force to political crimes, for instance.' He looked around and saw a great many faces all wearing the same expression, an expression stating that they were never going to be surprised by anything in history and that they had already had every thought that was ever going to be in his head. 'I think she means it's a hard, an exacting connexion to make,' he pushed on, 'this connexion between moral behaviour and political behaviour.... With a moral question, you ask yourself whether you can go on living as yourself if you do such and such a thing. But that isn't politics. It's self-conservation.' The woman made a pile of cracked Minton tea plates in the wire in-tray that she used for stacking the washing-up. 'It doesn't *work* very well as politics. Though you're bound to try to make it work, I do see,'' he said, watching her hands, 'in a place where opportunism's gone mad and grown so repulsive as a political dynamic.'

'Blimey,' said Annabel. 'Anyway, when wasn't it repulsive?'

'I hadn't finished.' He looked at her face and tried harder to speak for her. To her, perhaps. 'People before us.... Other times accepted it. They always found it natural in government. Opportunism was what kept politics going. America may be.... It's the suicidal greatness of America, I think Annabel means, to have raised opportunism to such a point that even people who wouldn't dream of ditching anything else feel that this has to be plucked out. Which is politically much like trying to run your old car without petrol.'

'I *suppose* that was what I meant,' said Annabel.

He took her away. 'What is it?' he said. 'I hated what I was saying, too.'

'You undercut too much.'

'There's no need to listen to me. Even I don't, altogether.'

'Yes, you do. You're in a bad way, aren't you? You don't know what next.'

'Spit in the face of the century?' he said.

'I'm frozen, 'she said. 'What's the poor century done?'

He blew seven shillings on a taxi to get them home in comfort, and she seemed glad to hold his hand. 'It's very nice to see you,' he said. 'Are you all right?' He meant, among other things, are you living with anyone, and she knew it, but she cared too much for the day together to tell him one way or the other.

'Where are the children?' he said. 'You haven't sent them to boarding school?'

'Are you out of your mind?' she said. 'I usually have one under each arm.'

'Where were you going? I forgot to ask.'

'I need some tights,' she said. He stopped the taxi at a shop and they bought tights at speed while the meter ticked.

'Could I see them? The kids?' he said when they had got back to his digs.

'Yes. Shall we have something to eat? Have you got any baked beans?' she said, to his joy. The tins were hidden behind a shelf of books because his landlady forbade cooking in the room, apart from kettle-boiling. 'You nit,' Annabel said. 'Behind the books is the first place she'll hunt.' They ate with a shared teaspoon out of the tin and she looked at the sardines and condensed milk now exposed between John Donne and Rosa Luxemburg.

'What?' Stephen said, worried.

'It's like tea caddies. All burglars know that ninety-eight per cent of all housewives decide to hide things in the tea caddy.' Stephen was felled by the things she knew. She passed him the tin and the spoon, and lay on the floor looking at the gas fire, and then she went to sleep. I was here once, he thought, stirred by a recollection that was not at all like an ordinary memory but more like a flash of *déjà vu* about some great happiness known before he was born. 'This is what it was like,' he said to himself. 'I have been here.'

When she woke, he was looking at the fire and reading P. G. Wodehouse.

'What are you thinking about?' she said.

'Wodehouse,' he said.

'What else?'

'Food, loot, you, and also me. And also what to do.'

'In what way?'

He kept quiet. He had been wondering where political allies might be, if anywhere. He suddenly saw that she was crying, though she said it was because of looking at the fire.

'Wouldn't you like to go and get the children and come

to stay here for a night or two?' he said. 'We could fit in somehow.'

'The landlady would have an attack.'

'I'd like it very much,' He paused. 'I could tell her I'd sleep in the bathroom.' He paused again. 'I could even *really* sleep in the bathroom, if you like.'

'Is it your own? Don't you share it?'

'The other bed-sitter's empty.'

'And she wouldn't let you sleep *there* overnight? No, I suppose not, old cow. Is she a cow, this one?'

'No.'

Annabel held her head. 'Darling, what am I blathering about? It's quite unrealistic to think of. I've got to go to a meeting. I should have been back at the office. It was my *lunch hour*. It's half past four.'

'Not worth going back,' Stephen said cheerfully. 'Will you get the sack?'

'No. I might have to sack myself. It's that sort of place. Oneself and one's conscience and the filing cabinets. You're out on trust, like a spaniel.'

A little later, she said, 'Come to the meeting with me. You might feel at home, I think. And then I honestly will have to go away.'

He felt her eluding him and said, 'What are you hiding?'

'I'm in love with someone. You obviously knew that, though. I'm living with him on and off. Mostly on, with luck. Called Charlie. You'll meet him if you come this evening. You'd like him.'

He was irritated by a piece of smut on her cheek and started to wipe it off, and then pretended he had been stroking her, because he saw her distress at an emotion that she had guessed with her usual impossible correctness. He took her to her meeting. She told him on the bus, nerving herself, that the children were Charlie's but that she had undertaken of her own accord not to tell anyone else because Charlie was the sort of person who couldn't be lumbered.

'Lumbered?' Stephen said only. Wait, breathe, start again.

'He's always going away. I suppose he has to. Does he? The thing is, I never believe he's going to come back. I couldn't tell anyone else this. It's not painful to hear, is it? My dear friend.'

'That's the trouble with women and dogs,' Stephen said furiously, heart splitting for a second, because it was also the trouble with himself, now and then. 'They never believe you're going to come back. They don't know the meaning of soon.'

'Isn't the same thing true of you?' she said. 'Of men?'

'I'm not a man, I'm a phenomenon,' he said, with no expression.

'Who isn't?' she managed. She heard that he was speaking wretchedly, not arrogantly, but it would have been a patronage to recognize that any further, and she had to let him be rancorous.

The meeting was in a Notting Hill flat. The room was full of young men talking politics and being affably rude to each other. They wore clothes that he thought beautiful, when he could see for envy: jackets with Napoleonic pockets, trousers cut so that they reached the ground at the back, pink shirts, print ties. There were a few girls there. One of the young men had been hurt in a demonstration and his clothes were spattered with his blood. He was holding his left eye. His girl leaned over him, talking to him, with her long straight hair swinging over his face. In a corner of the room there was a mimeograph machine. A girl and a man were working it, faces transparent from fatigue. Cheery posters hung on the wall, and there were a lot of tables shaped like children's bricks that did for stools or in-trays, made of clear Perspex and spotted with dabs of red and blue paint. Annabel tried to persuade Stephen to join her on a bright-blue canvas swing seat with Charlie. Stephen had already taken in two things: that he was with a set of people he would have liked very much to belong to, and that Annabel was hitched to a man who treated her idly. The two observations did not go well with each other. Like most strong men in an extreme of daze and hurt, he spoke many unnecessary words. One or two of the people he spoke to found him politically fascinating, even if they did take his style of callous irony with no irony of their own. They spoke of him later rather generously. Stephen left as soon as possible, maintaining brusqueness.

He had a cup of tea with his landlady before he went to bed. Felix had tracked him down through his old address and left a note. That cheered him. The landlady, Mrs Jenkins, was married to a fifty-five-year-old man who drove a vegetable lorry. He kept dropping off in their presence because he went to work at three every morning.

'This is a country that should export,' Mrs Jenkins said. 'We always seem to be importing and I don't know why. We'll be devalued again and any fool but the government can see it coming, can't they? Alfred, you shouldn't eat that.'

'Why not?' said Mr Jenkins, wide awake with the cheek of it and now taking not one but two pieces of her best fruit cake.

'The doctor says it's harmful to you.'

'Doctors have been the cause of many people dying.'

'Well, Mr Brandt,' said Mrs Jenkins, turning, 'I don't know what your politics are, but we're old trades-union people and I'm disappointed. We should export more, as I was saying. That's what all the papers keep telling them and yet none of them take a blind bit of notice. Governments are paid to know things like that. To think quicker than us. It's not our job, after all. Yet it seems they keep doing the wrong thing at the wrong time, according to the papers. It'd make me pack it in and go to Canada if I was younger, but you can't leave England, can you?' She poured some more tea. 'This monkeying around. It's bad for the country. It's a worry, isn't it?'

'I'm half Viennese, you know. I'm only half English.'

'But you've always lived here.' She adjusted to something hopeful.

'Since I was eighteen. I usually call myself half German because people get so fed up with all the Germans who say they're Austrian.'

'Well, I don't suppose it was easy, the war, wherever you were. Mr Jenkins and I had a very nice friend who came from Italy. He spoke perfect English, like yourself.'

Stephen read for hours upstairs. People manage on short commons, he thought in the middle of his book. He dreamed of the blooded face with the girl's hair swinging over it, and of Annabel's children, and then he surfaced again and went for a walk through Covent Garden fruit market, where Mr Jenkins must already be at work. There was the usual fine smell from the apples spilled and crushed in the gutter. He contemplated eating a meat pie at the stall by the church, but he had enough experience of phantom hunger at night to know that it would disappear of its own accord by morning and that it was best not to squander money on appeasing it. He went to bed and dreamed again. Two old-age pensioners were dancing in a ballroom lit by chandeliers. They were jostled by smart young people, and no one would do anything for them. It's the bad hour of the night, he thought, awake. Mrs Jenkins seemed to be in the room, looking sad. Excuse me, he thought, addressing himself to her, excuse me if I'm being personal, but when was your last laugh? Not long ago, she said in his head, one comes to rely on one's bit of fun, and he tried her with a joke or two, but the old happy creasing of the face took time to occur. Then Annabel, actual Annabel, broke into the night by throwing gravel up at his wondow to attract his attention. She looked strange. She had the children with her. It seemed that she had had a row with her man and that he had left.

'For good?'

'More or less. It's always more or less. This time I made it happen, I think.' Her voice was blurred.

The children were jolly enough. They trundled about the room looking at things and then sat behind one another on his bed and played train carriages.

'They should be asleep, shouldn't they?' Stephen said, and the five-year-old said, 'No, of course not, it's today now.'

'They'll never go off now that it's light. I'm going to be

sick.' Annabel staggered out of the door and he followed her. She sat on the rim of the bath and then fell on to the floor. She wouldn't speak or open her eyes, and he shook her very hard.

'I was asleep,' she said thickly.

'Are you drunk?'

'I've taken sleeping pills. Only two. I only wanted to go to sleep.' She started to get hysterical and self-pitying. 'I've run out of money and I'm trapped with the children and I don't like it here. It's a bad time.'

'Don't gripe. Change it.'

'You've got energy. You're remarkable. It's different for you.'

'Change it.'

She opened her eyes and glared at him. 'All very well to say. You don't know what it's like.'

'No?'

'Don't be sarcastic. I didn't mean you've got much, except this energy. I only meant you're more used to it.' The children shouted next door and Annabel covered her ears and said, 'I can't.'

'That's not true of yourself.'

'I just can't. I want to go to sleep for a month. I don't like any of it. I hate my rotten job and I'm still not earning enough and I don't see the kids enough and there aren't enough people like you with enough of whatever it is to change anything. None of it's enough.' She went to sleep, and woke to growl, 'Me least,' and he put a bath towel round her and tried to carry her into his bed-sitting-room, but he was too frail to do it and she had to wake up again to walk by herself. She opened one eye and grinned at him. The children were playing the theatre-organ on his type-writer and chatting to each other. It seemed such a good morning in many ways that he was prompted to an unbearable hope and said, 'Would you ever marry me?'

'Perhaps I could stay here for a day or two,' she said. But she had to reply. 'I'm a tramp. Both kinds. Tramps shouldn't marry. I'm not in love with you.' There was another pause, and then she said, 'Maybe,' which he knew for no.

She went to sleep for a respite, and when she woke up Stephen was in draughty self-possession. He was holding one of the children, who was asleep. 'Look,' he said, trying to help her. 'You're born nobody and on your own. So you've nothing to lose, have you? It's not a bad position to strike from.'

Penelope Gilliatt

An Antique Love Story

'The walls aren't vulnerable to dents,' said the head of the office, leading a guided tour in a New York summer dusk. 'What we have here is reinforced concrete.' He led these tours each Thursday, after working hours.

Amy and I are a bit alike, thought a messenger boy called Ed. (His major work was the turning on and off of the lights every Thursday evening.) The likeness may lie mostly in shutting up. (He looked at the people in front of him, being shown round the modern office, exclaiming.) What if she overrates me? I'm not in love with her, he thought. I never miss her when I'm not with her. (Though then he day-dreamed of her in bed. Speechless.)

'We think we have something quite new here in walls,' said the head of the office, who had been talking all the while. He made a flourish at the concrete.

A Lady Mayoress from England – Ed's country and Amy's – found a nail file in her bag and tried to scratch the wall, and then took off her shoe and banged the wall gaily with the heel. 'Such a lot of walls now are hardboard,' she said to the office head. 'These are concrete.'

'Yes, these are reinforced concrete,' the head of the office said. 'We have something here that's not vulnerable to dents. And this' – moving on – 'is the main work area.' Ed spent the day in the work area. He was twenty-four. There was cork on the floor and the ceiling. Everything – walls, floor, ceiling, desks – was in filing-cabinet grey. The Coke

63

machine was in filing-cabinet grey, with mushroom-beige panels and brown doughnuts. It had been specially sprayed.

'This *city*,' said a businessman on the tour, slumping into a desk chair and talking to no one in particular. 'I like living in New York, I tell you. Culture-wise, there's no city with half as much. Is there? Theatre-wise. Transportation-wise. Buildings. Restaurants. You can't do better any place in the world. Limousines. Who *cares* about the dirt?' But here he rubbed his hand through his hair and then inspected his fingers, which were grey; and he shuddered at the three-day deposit of New York smog, and looked resentful.

A tired section manager stared out of the window and bit his fingernails. 'Yup, it's the energy,' he said. 'On the go. I tell you, this office is like Grand Central Station when it's on the go.' He gazed round the office, not savouring its emptiness after hours. There was a secondhand copy of Webster's English Dictionary open on a lectern. The architect had put it there as a last touch. Nobody ever looked anything up in it. It was the only old thing in the place. The secretaries had secretarial dictionaries to use if they ever needed them, but most of the girls were on computers. 'I guess this place is beautiful when it's on the go,' the section manager said.

'Well, it's a beautiful building,' said the Lady Mayoress.

'Lived in,' said the section manager. He patted a counter gratefully. 'These are a wonderful height. These counters.'

'In so far as our thinking is concerned,' the head of the office said, 'I believe I can say that our motivation, part of our motivation, is in the area of providing the work force with a work, er, area, that will meet their human needs.'

A distinguished European visitor, a woman, mustered herself against him.

'We're watching now for results,' the office head went on. 'We've put a lot of thought into this. I'll be very interested to see how the work force responds.'

Ed slipped away to his own desk and took a Kleenex out of the drawer. If I get rich, he thought, one of the first things I'll do will be to go back to linen handkerchiefs. It's the only thing I miss about the past, he thought firmly, although he was in the midst of staring around the office and hating it.

'The place we used to be in was pretty run down, I'll tell you that,' the head of the office said. 'Now we've made this effort and we're beginning to see results. It was an effort, all right, but I'm happy to say it's paying off.'

The group moved ahead. Ed turned on a farther set of lights and turned off the ones behind.

'There's a gathering of strength,' the office head went on to the visitors. The section manager, pleased, stopped biting his fingernails and then slouched exhaustedly into some-one's desk chair. 'There's a new vigour,' said the office head.

'You'd have got the same effect if you'd cleaned up the old cloakrooms,' the distinguished European woman mut-tered. Ed heard her; he generally caught remarks that went by other people. A sort of fatuous cheerfulness seemed to him to govern most talkers, and he had an ear for the softly mutinous.

He wandered off, feeling underpaid and acutely hungry. He spent most of his wages on rent and wine and books. He often found and ate whole delicatessen meals thrown away in the office rubbish baskets. The amount of usable garbage in New York astonished him. This evening, for instance, when the tour party had left, he salvaged a per-fectly good cold hamburger out of the wastebasket of a sec-retary he liked. The act quite cheered him, though the food was a little disgusting.

He rang Amy up. They began with their own silence. After some time, Amy said, 'Hang on while I get a cigarette.'

Wait until she comes back. There she is. Friendly pause – what else? Wait again. What are we? Fond. Yes.

'It's nice you rang up,' Amy said.

'Yes.'

Pause.

'I don't want to talk about my life and I don't want to make small talk,' he said. Pause. 'Like you.' Pause. 'As you know.'

Pause.

'Is it hard on you?' he said.

Pause.

'What?' said Amy.

'Me not talking?'

After a longer pause, she laughed like anything and said, 'What are you blathering about?'

When he got home he found her washing her hair. It hung usually in a plait that was long enough to sit on. They tried to go to sleep later among the damp strands, which spread everywhere. She woke in the middle of the night several times, spluttering because she had hair in her mouth. At four o'clock she got up. 'It's like the Sargasso Sea,' she said, plaiting. 'It's like going to sleep in weeds.' Ed watched her. She came back into bed and laid the damp plait carefully over the edge of the mattress. 'I should have done that before,' she said.

'I'm hungry,' he said. 'I like your plait.'

'What about some cold toad-in-the-hole?' she said.

'It's nice now,' he said, half an hour later. 'It wasn't a good evening early on.'

They had a silence, eating and reading, and then she said, 'I think happy may really mean interested.'

'People mostly seem to keep *pretending* to be interested.'

'That's what's been bothering you.'

'Or else there's nothing there at all and they have to invent something,' he said. 'Everyone's talking to himself. Was it ever like this before? What are you thinking about?'

'That. Oh, and also not being keen on what I look like. I can see myself from here. It doesn't matter.'

'You're beautiful. You look like Amy.'

'Perhaps I should try a fringe. Would you mind?'

'Up to you. Don't spoil your face, that's all.'

She looked at him curiously. 'What does my face consist of?'

They lived in a poor part of New York. Politicians called it 'disadvantaged'. They had two rooms. A child named

Izolska lived down the hall. She had a Polish-Jewish father, recently widowed, who drove a taxi. The child spent most of every day on the floor above, with a retired old actress named Mrs Green, because there was no school in the neighbourhood for her to go to. So long as Mrs Green was alone with Izolska, she would watch her and give her dried pieces of fruitcake out of a big tin with Roosevelt's portrait on it, but when anyone else was there she would take cover in senile imaginings and refer to herself in the third person as Astrid-Agnes, after two sisters in a story she had read long ago. At other moments of threat she would say that she was God, knitting angrily and fending off questions.

On Friday, when Amy had left for work, Ed thought of throwing in his job to get on with something better. He had a telephone. He looked at it, and at the papers and library books on his desk (three planks on two trestles), and contemplated making a telephone call to offer himself full time to an amnesty movement he had once helped. And then he sheered away from commitment, and went to see Mrs Green instead. Her knitting lay beside her, and she was talking to Izolska, who was due for a lesson by phone with a computer.

'Why aren't you at work?' Izolska said to Ed.

'Isn't it time for your arithmetic lesson?' Ed countered.

'Lessons on the telephone! They call that modern!' Mrs Green shouted, reaching out to get her knitting for fear she would need it, but holding the child by the skirt with her other hand.

'I just thought I wouldn't go to work today,' Ed said.

'You'll be fired,' said Izolska.

'Well,' said Ed, 'yes.' He looked at Mrs Green, whose hand was still clutching Izolska's skirt. 'Would you like her to have the lesson here?' he said to the old lady.

'She doesn't have a telephone, Ed,' the child said. She contemplated adult blunders. 'You two have the only one in the house, except Louie, and his place smells.'

Mrs Green started knitting.

'I forgot. Hadn't we better be going? Isn't it time?' Ed said to Izolska.

'Not till eleven. You know, you don't have to sit with me,' Izolska said. 'I can use the door key fine on my own. I've done it lots of times.'

'I'd like to hear the lesson. I never have,' Ed said. Izolska looked at her Pop Art watch, which her father had given her last year on her eighth birthday. Mrs Green knitted more intensely.

'What are you knitting, Mrs Green?' Ed said.

Mrs Green lifted the needles, working all the time, and made the sign of the Cross over him with them.

'What are you knitting, Lord?' he said.

'Human organs. Essential organs.'

'I should think Izolska will come back here after the lesson,' Ed said.

'Hearts, lungs, wombs,' she said, keeping her eyes on the needles and not raising them as Izolska left.

Ed offered the little girl a Coke in his apartment, but she refused and sat by the push-button phone in a way that made him feel he should go into the other room. He lay on the bed and smoked. She put a piece of paper and a pencil beside the telephone and doodled something, and then looked at her watch and sat still for five minutes, checking her watch several times before she punched the number of an office called Touch-Tone-Tuition, which had given her an appointment with a computer. The telephone voice must have told her she had done something wrong, for she put the receiver down fast and then the telephone rang her back. She punched out an identification number and was put through to the computer. The computer asked a question in a voice that Ed could hear. Izolska punched out 1–5–6 on the telephone.

'Correct,' said the computer after an eerie halt, going straight on to its next problem. When she was right, the computer would put another question within one second. She was right consecutively for three-and-a-half minutes. Then she began being wrong. In that case, the computer was programmed to repeat the question. If she gave the wrong answer again, it told her the right one and went on to another problem. This happened five times. Izolska started holding her hand against her left ear, although there was no noise in the room. After she had put down the telephone she shook like a little dog for a second. She asked for a Coke.

Ed got one out of the cupboard. Amy kept food there because it was the coldest place in the apartment. 'It doesn't look much fun,' he said. 'It looks hard.'

'The computer can't explain, you see,' she said.

He asked her if she wanted to tell him the questions that had stumped her, hoping to help her, but she was learning the system called the New Math, and his own old way of working out the answers only confused her. So then they had a game of two-handed poker, which cheered her up. She left politely after a while, and went to play with a ball against the wall with some other children in the street.

He lay in a chair to read, and remembered her on the telephone, and then he thought about Amy and himself. I don't miss her. I don't want to marry her. I never think about her when I'm alone, he thought, thinking about her. I don't give her much. I behave like some forebear of the robot. (Hell.) I can throw up my job just like that. There's always something else. I could lose Amy, if I had to. (Unhappy.) A little read would be reviving, in the circumstances. He lay on his back. After an hour he jerked out of the book like a stranded fish, and struggled, and thought again of Izolska's hand against her ear on the telephone to the computer, and then of Amy and of whether he was behaving like a computer to her. He went out fast into the street and took the subway to the office where Amy worked, circling around the block and telling himself that he hadn't particularly got her in mind. Then he bought two paperbacks and went into a cafeteria for coffee. And Amy was there, at the head of the queue. He watched her with her tray. He saw her eye the tables and make for one that had a lot of food left on it, with no waitress close enough to clear the plates away before she had commandeered them. Living on leftovers was something he understood, but he had always thought himself alone in that economy. It struck him to the bone to see Amy heading for an uneaten roll and half a piece of pie.

He reached the end of the queue and put the tray down on to another table, standing with the cup of coffee in his hand and wondering what to do. She was wearing her plait down her back today. She ate from the two plates briefly and then pushed them away and looked for something in her bag. A dime. She made for a phone booth. He came up behind her and tapped her on the shoulder, and she spun round and said, 'I was just going to telephone you.' They sat down together and enjoyed themselves, barely talking. They went home later on a bus together.

'Something happened to you today,' Amy said.

'Yes,' he said.

'But we don't have to have a conversation,' she said.

The man on Amy's other side, a middle-aged man with ragged hair and an interested face, prodded her knee with the end of the rolled-up New York *Post*, just as Ed was looking at her and saying, 'Thank heaven for you.'

'There's no doubt, of course, that the soul is female,' the stranger said.

'Shut up,' Ed said softly.

'The soul is female. One goes to it for advice,' said the stranger, who did not look mad. He fixed Amy with a stare.

'Do you?' she said.

'I shall dream about you, and my unconscious will decide what I think of you,' he said. 'It may decide you haven't been listening to a word I've been saying. It may decide I want to have an affair with you. Do you believe in reincarnation? I am related to earlier kings of the English and the French. This is why I speak with an English accent. I can tell you are both English. You notice I don't say "British". I believe the fact of the French incarnations to be the reason for my collecting French furniture. When funds allow.'

Ed took Amy's bag and looked inside it, needing something to do. The man rumpled his hair forward with his hand and said, 'I'm afraid I'm a man who often bores people. I don't notice it. You must meet my wife.'

'Yes,' Ed said.

'Do you live together?' the man asked, following them to the exit of the bus. He put his foot between the closing doors so as to hear their answer, and the driver shouted at him.

'Yes,' said Ed.

Amy stayed up late reading Simenon, and turned on the portable TV that Ed had borrowed. The news wasn't very good to hear. Then she looked at a movie with Humphrey Bogart, and filled in a form for a visa. She was planning a trip to Europe. Ed was lying awake in the bedroom and he watched her for a couple of hours. After a time, he saw her stomping around with her hands in the pockets of her jeans and a cigarette hanging out of her mouth, and he understood that she must be practising a Bogey slouch.

By three in the morning she was in bed asleep and Ed was still awake. He got up to take two aspirins and one stuck in his windpipe. The pain reminded him of being a child and of swallowing boiled sweets that he had tucked into his cheek to try to spin them out. Choking, he wondered whether he would die, and balked at that, and choked some more, holding the table and idly reading Amy's visa form through the coughing fit. She had stopped filling it in at the question 'In the case of injury or death, whom should the authorities inform?' The name she had started to give, stopping halfway through the address, was her own. Moved, he paced the apartment. It was a warm night. At six o'clock, when he had finished his book and taken to trying sleep on the floor so as not to wake Amy up – *programming* himself to sleep, he put it to himself, because wakefulness was clearly unfunctional and not fitting to the nature he thought he had – there was a knock at the door. There stood Bill, an old latcher-on who suffered twinges of paranoia late at night and roamed the city for acquaintances to attack with his insomnia.

'I knew you'd be up,' Bill said, flying in the face of the evidence of bedclothes on the floor and an Ed barely dressed. They sat for a time. Ed could think of nothing to say, and of even less reason than usual to try. It seemed to him that he had been hearing many sorely awry efforts to talk. 'Would you like a drink?' he managed at last.

'I knew you'd be awake,' Bill said, glaring, and getting up to bore a finger into Ed's chest. 'See here. I've something to say to you, buddy.'

'Buddy?' said Ed. I scarcely know the man, he thought.

'I've something to say to you,' Bill said. The finger pressed. 'My nature doesn't allow me to conceal from you my opinion that you've behaved like a bastard to me. A bastard.'

'What?'

'I came up here specially to see you, right? And yet you've deliberately never come to see me. What's more, you didn't ask me here.'

'No,' Ed said mildly.

'You admit it.'

'Well, I'm very sorry, old boy, but I didn't mean anything by it.' Ed concentrated uninterruptedly on the way Bill was now standing. He had his hand in his right pocket. Ed realized that he had a revolver in there.

'All I am to you is an acquaintance,' Bill said, in the most alarming voice. 'You make that clear enough. You treat me the way the British treated the Indians they did business with. Did they ever ask them into their homes? Not on your life. You bet. That's what I mean.'

'But we *are* acquaintances. We barely know each other.'

Bill laughed bitterly. 'That's just what I mean,' he said.

Ed was invaded by holy calm and started counting on his fingers the possible number of hours' sleep left to him, given the good luck that Bill lost interest in murdering him and sloped off.

'Some friend,' Bill said, helping himself to a drink.

Ed counted hours of sleep again.

'What are you doing?' Bill said, in a voice sharp as ice.

'Counting,' said Ed.

'Counting what?'

Ed saw the physical provocation in replying 'Hours of sleep,' and said nothing.

'Counting what?' The revolver inside the pocket was pointing at him.

'Practising scales, actually. Playing the piano,' Ed said in hope.

Bill glared, and startlingly dozed. There is some mercy, Ed thought.

Next morning, a Saturday, Ed woke at noon and found himself alone and alive with Amy, who was laughing.

'Do you know what I did?' she said, giving him a cup of coffee. 'I was filling in a form and started writing down me as the person to get in touch with if I · · s dead.'

'I saw,' he said, touching her nose. 'It made me sad at the time.'

'No, it's funny.'

'Did you know that I nearly died last night? Bill blundered in at six in the morning and he had a revolver in his pocket that he was going to use on me because he hadn't been asked to come. People do odd things on Friday nights.'

Ed thought of himself as a man with no gift for weekends. It was part of his robot vision. He believed that, with luck, he knew how to use his own spare time functionally, but other people's seemed too much to dispose of well. Other people reposed too much trust. Other people wanted to go on outings and picnics that he might easily bungle. Other people tried so hard to believe that weekends must be bound to be better than their weeks had been. Who were these other people, though? That morning, he thought of families sitting in cars by the summer highways, eating picnics to the roar of cars exactly like their own, and then he decided that these probably weren't the people he meant, to be fair. Entertaining no great sense of superiority to anyone, he borrowed a car and drove Mrs Green and Izolska and Amy to the country. With the gathering of the four of them, life growingly seemed gay and splendid. Although the age managed to put its comic oar in. Amy had to get out of the car to telephone the airport about a booking. They stopped at a garage. Ed listened in the booth.

'I want to confirm a reservation,' she said. She gave her name. She had to plug her left ear, like Izolska, against the noise of the traffic.

'Sorry, Ma'am, but our computers are in malfunction.'

'What?'

'You'll have to call again. We are unable to confirm your reservation at this time.'

'Can't say either yes or no?'

'That understanding is correct, lady.'

'When shall I telephone again, then?'

'If you'll call again in one hour to one-and-one-half hours, our computers will be glad to speak with you.'

In the car, Ed held the end of Amy's plait as he drove. Izolska sat between them. Mrs Green, in the back, had brought with her a tapestry cushion cover that she was making. Amy turned round in the car and leaned her chin on the seat, like a tall dog propping its jawbone on the edge of a bed. Izolska hummed. They found a river and had a picnic beside it. Silence and interest gradually merged into a formidable hope in Ed's head, and he felt he had a bead on his life. Clicking a bottle against his teeth, he watched Mrs Green listening to the news on his car radio. The car was parked thirty feet from where they were sitting. Mrs Green sat on the front passenger seat with the door open, her feet on the ground and her head down, listening. She troubled over events in the world and had no trust in the President. She came back without words, and started to work furiously on her tapestry cushion.

'We all have these thoughts sometimes,' Ed said.

Amy asked what the President had said.

Mrs Green stitched. Izolska jumped into the river, holding her nose. 'There are some human beings who do not wish for immortality at all,' said Mrs Green.

Amy swore at the President.

'No, we have to put up with the fact that people will always say and do things we find unforgivably disappoint-

ing,' said Mrs Green. 'Do you care for this blue, or not?
At the same time we have to preserve enough of the sense of
outrage to change things. Are you two short of the sense of
outrage?'

'No,' Ed said.

'Only on Saturdays,' said Amy.

'I wish you weren't going away,' he said to her.

'It's only for a few weeks.'

'Away?' said Mrs Green.

'Amy's going home to England, and then she wants to go
to Czechoslovakia.'

'You'll be back soon.' Mrs Green opened her eyes wider
as she said this and stitched hard at the tapestry.

'In a few weeks.'

Mrs Green here closed her eyes and said, 'Leaving us.'

'No, I'll be back. I live here now. Does anyone want a
rest? Are you tired?'

'I don't want a rest. I've never liked rests. What a pity the
longest day's gone. I always enjoy that. Still, October can be
crackerjack. Look at that, now. Just enough of the green
wool to finish. Well done. The week will yet be a success.'

A butterfly came near, attracted by the colours of the
tapestry. Ed held Amy's hand.

'You may be leaving him for too long,' Mrs Green said.
'Although Czechoslovakia's an interesting place.'

'Did you ever act there?' Ed said. 'When did you give
up the stage? Amy, I'm definitely going to pack it in at the
office. I shan't be making much money. Will you support
us?'

'Thank you,' she said. 'Thank you for asking.'

'I'm not very good at it. Mrs Green, sorry, I was interested, actually. Czechoslovakia. Did you ever act there?'

'It's not easy, asking for things,' Amy said to Ed, and
then to Mrs Green, 'After Vienna?'

'I was told at fifty that I should stop,' Mrs Green said.
'That was in London after the tour. They said I was in my
prime. They thought I should end it there. Well, there were
character parts I'd have liked to have played, but one

night I decided they were probably right. It wouldn't have done. I realized it the night I had to put on my glasses to see to cut up my meat.' She paused. 'It was on my birthday. There was a splendid party. You could call that a tonic event.'

There was a congenial silence.

'You know I've only got one eye left now,' Mrs Green said.

Ed said 'Sh-h-h' to Izolska, who was splashing them.

'Did I wet you?' she said.

'Nearly,' Ed said.

'There are people who don't like me, now no one knows who I was. I can understand that. Still, I don't worry,' said Mrs Green.

Amy said, 'Some people have an instinct ahead. Ed has. You have. Other people have an instinct behind. And then there are others who are exactly in step and they'll obviously always be the ones who get on. They hardly have to open their mouths before everyone recognizes his own thoughts.'

Mrs Green packed up her tapestry. She had not talked of herself as Astrid-Agnes or as God all day. She crossed her legs and formed her fingers into a telescope and put them to her seeing eye, squinting at a tree.

'I lost my eye, you see, and that's why I don't have a television. I like the radio. Watching television is like having an electric current put through the good eye and that's no help, is it? The authorities would give me a television set for nothing, but I can't stand it because it makes this good eye tremble and that's no help to anyone, is it? As I said before.'

Izolska watched the butterfly. 'It likes the colours of my wool,' Mrs Green said. Izolska started splashing again and sang a song to an out-of-tune yell of her own. 'My pretty pretty butterfly, come over here, it's Saturday,' she howled, raising her head like a street singer baying at the sky in front of a cinema queue. I like it here, thought Amy. I like it here, thought Ed. The beloved child should be quiet, thought Mrs Green. '*Basta*,' the child told herself, out loud.

'Well,' said Mrs Green, 'I'm afraid you've known me in the lesser years. It's time that does it. However, today sees me revived.'

Ed took Amy away by the river and said, with his hand around her neck, 'Would you be back for good, possibly?'

Benedict Kiely

A Ball of Malt and Madame Butterfly

On a warm but not sunny June afternoon on a crowded
Dublin street, by no means one of the city's most elegant
streets, a small hotel, a sort of bed-and-breakfast place,
went on fire. There was pandemonium at first, more panic
than curiosity in the crowd. It was a street of decayed
Georgian houses, high and narrow, with steep wooden stair-
cases, and cluttered small shops on the ground floors: all
great nourishment for flames. The fire, though, didn't turn
out to be serious. The brigade easily contained and con-
trolled it. The panic passed, gave way to curiosity, then to
indignation and finally, alas, to laughter about the odd
thing that had happened when the alarm was at its worst.

This was it.

From a window on the topmost floor a woman, scantily
clad, puts her head out and waves a patchwork bed-
coverlet, and screams for help. The stairway, she cries, is
thick with smoke, herself and her husband are afraid to
face it. On what would seem to be prompting from inside
the room, she calls down that they are a honeymoon couple
up from the country. That would account fairly enough for
their still being abed on a warm June afternoon.

The customary ullagone and ullalu goes up from the
crowd. The fire-engine ladder is aimed up to the window. A
fireman begins to run up the ladder. Then suddenly the
groom appears in shirt and trousers, and barefooted. For, to
the horror of the beholders, he makes his bare feet visible by

Benedict Kiely

pushing the bride back into the room, clambering first out the window, down the ladder like a monkey although he is a fairly corpulent man and, with catlike agility, dodging round the ascending fireman, then disappearing through the crowd. The people, indignant enough to trounce him, are still too concerned with the plight of the bride, and too astounded, to seize him. The fireman ascends to the nuptial casement, helps the lady through the window and down the ladder, gallantly offering his jacket which covers some of her. Then when they are halfway down, the fireman to the amazement of all is seen to be laughing right merrily, the bride vituperating. But before they reach the ground she also is laughing. She is brunette, tall, but almost Japanese in appearance, and very handsome. A voice says: If she's a bride I can see no confetti in her hair.

She has fine legs which the fireman's jacket does nothing to conceal and which she takes pride, clearly, in displaying. She is a young woman of questionable virginity and well-known to the firemen. She is the toast of a certain section of the town to whom she is affectionately known as Madame Butterfly, although unlike her more famous namesake she has never been married nor cursed by an uncle Bonze for violating the laws of the gods of her ancestors. She has another, registered name: her mother's name. What she is, her mother was before her, and proud of it.

The barefooted fugitive was not, of course, a bridegroom, but a long-established married man with his wife and family and a prosperous business in Longford, the meanest town in Ireland. For the fun of it the firemen made certain that the news of his escapade in the June afternoon got back to Longford. They were fond of, even proud of Butterfly, as were many other men who had nothing at all to do with the quenching of fire.

But one man loved the pilgrim soul in her and his name was Pike Hunter.

Like Borgnefesse, the buccaneer of St Malo on the Rance, who had a buttock shot or sliced off in action on the Spanish

80

Main, Pike Hunter had a lopsided appearance when sitting down. Standing up he was as straight and well-balanced as a man could be: a higher civil servant approaching the age of forty, a shy bachelor, reared, nourished and guarded all his life by a trinity of upper-middle-class aunts. He was pink-faced, with a little fair hair left to emphasize early baldness, mild in his ways, with a slight stutter, somewhat afraid of women. He wore always dark-brown suits with a faint red stripe, dark-brown hats, rimless spectacles, shiny square-toed brown handmade shoes with a wide welt. In summer, even on the hottest day, he carried a raincoat folded over his arm, and a rolled umbrella. When it rained he unfolded and wore the raincoat and opened and raised the umbrella. He suffered mildly from hay-fever. In winter he belted himself into a heavy brown overcoat and wore galoshes. Nobody ever had such stiff white shirts. He favoured brown neckties distinguished with a pearl-headed pin. Why he sagged to one side, just a little to the left, when he sat down, I never knew. He had never been sliced or shot on the Spanish Main.

But the chance of a sunny, still, Sunday afternoon in Stephen's Green and Grafton Street, the select heart or soul of the city's south side, made a changed man out of him.

He had walked at his ease through the Green, taking the sun gratefully, blushing when he walked between the rows of young ladies lying back in deck-chairs. He blushed for two reasons: they were reclining, he was walking; they were as gracefully at rest as the swans on the lake, he was awkwardly in motion, conscious that his knees rose too high, that his sparse hair – because of the warmth he had his hat in his hand – danced long and ludicrously in the little wind, that his shoes squeaked. He was fearful that his right toe might kick his left heel, or vice versa, and that he would fall down and be laughed at in laughter like the sound of silver bells. He was also alarmingly aware of the bronze knees, and more than knees, that the young ladies exposed as they leaned back and relaxed in their light summer frocks. He would honestly have liked to stop and enumerate those

Benedict Kiely

knees, make an inventory – he was in the Department of Statistics: perhaps pat a few here and there. But the fearful regimen of that trinity of aunts forbade him even to glance sideways, and he stumbled on like a winkered horse, demented by the flashing to right and to left of bursting globes of bronze light.

Then on the park pathway before him walking towards the main gate and the top of Grafton Street, he saw the poet. He had seen him before, but only in the Abbey Theatre and never on the street. Indeed it seemed hardly credible to Pike Hunter that such a man would walk on the common street where all ordinary or lesser men were free to place their feet. In the Abbey Theatre the poet had all the strut and style of a man who could walk with the gods, the Greek gods that is, not the gods in the theatre's cheapest seats. His custom was to enter by a small stairway, at the front of the house and in full view of the audience, a few moments before the lights dimmed and the famous gong sounded and the curtain rose. He walked slowly, hands clasped behind his back, definitely balancing the prone brow oppressive with its mind, the eagle head aloft and crested with foaming white hair. He would stand, his back to the curtain and facing the house. The chatter would cease, the fiddlers in the orchestra would saw with diminished fury. Some of the city wits said that what the poet really did at those times was to count the empty seats in the house and make a rapid reckoning of the night's takings. But their gibe could not diminish the majesty of those entrances, the majesty of the stance of the man. And there he was now, hands behind back, noble head high, pacing slowly, beginning the course of Grafton Street. Pike Hunter walked behind him, suiting his pace to the poet's, to the easy deliberate rhythms of the early love poetry: I would that we were, my beloved, white birds on the foam of the sea. There is a queen in China or, maybe, it's in Spain.

They walked between the opulent windows of elegant glittering shops, doors closed for Sunday. The sunshine had

82

drawn the people from the streets: to the park, to the lush green country, to the seaside. Of the few people they did meet, not all of them seemed to know who the poet was, but those who did know saluted quietly, with a modest and unaffected reverence, and one young man with a pretty girl on his arm stepped off the pavement, looked after the poet and clearly whispered to the maiden who it was that had just passed by the way. Stepping behind him at a respectful distance Pike felt like an acolyte behind a celebrant and regretted that there was no cope or cloak of cloth of gold of which he could humbly carry the train.

So they sailed north towards the Liffey, leaving Trinity College, with Burke standing haughty-headed and Goldsmith sipping at his honeypot of a book, to the right, and the Bank and Grattan orating *Esto Perpetua*, to the left, and Thomas Moore of the Melodies, brown, stooped and shabby, to the right; and came unto Westmoreland Street where the wonder happened. For there approaching them came the woman Homer sung: old and grey and, perhaps, full of sleep, a face much and deeply lined and haggard, eyes sunken, yet still the face of the queen she had been when she and the poet were young and they had stood on the cliffs on Howth Head, high above the promontory that bears the Bailey Lighthouse as a warning torch and looks like the end of the world; and they had watched the soaring of the gulls and he had wished that he and she were only white birds, my beloved, buoyed out on the foam of the sea. She was very tall. She was not white, but all black in widow's weeds for the man she had married when she wouldn't marry the poet. Her black hat had a wide brim and, from the brim, an old-fashioned veil hung down before her face. The pilgrim soul in you, and loved the sorrows of your changing face.

Pike stood still, fearing that in a dream he had intruded on some holy place. The poet and the woman moved dreamlike towards each other, then stood still, not speaking, not saluting, at opposite street-corners where Fleet Street comes narrowly from the East to join Westmoreland Street.

Then still not speaking, not saluting, they turned into Fleet Street. When Pike tiptoed to the corner and peered around he saw that they had walked on opposite sides of the street for, perhaps, thirty paces, then turned at right angles, moved towards each other, stopped to talk in the middle of the street where a shaft of sunlight had defied the tall, overshadowing buildings. Apart from themselves and Pike that portion of the town seemed to be awesomely empty; and there Pike left them and walked in a daze by the side of the Liffey to a pub called the 'Dark Cow'. Something odd had happened to him: poetry, a vision of love?

It so happened that on that day Butterfly was in the 'Dark Cow' as, indeed, she often was: just Butterfly and Pike, and Jody with the red carbuncled face who owned the place and was genuinely kind to the girls of the town, and a few honest dockers who didn't count because they had money only for their own porter and were moral men, loyal to wives or sweethearts. It wasn't the sort of place Pike frequented. He had never seen Butterfly before: those odd slanting eyes, the glistening high-piled black hair, the well-defined bud of a mouth, the crossed legs, the knees that outclassed to the point of mockery all the bronze globes in Stephen's Green. Coming on top of his vision of the poet and the woman all this was too much for him, driving him to a reckless courage that would have flabbergasted the three aunts. He leaned on the counter. She sat in an alcove that was a sort of throne for her, where on busier days she sat surrounded by her sorority. So he says to Jody whom he did not yet know as Jody: May I have the favour of buying the lady in the corner a drink?

– That you may, and more besides.

– Please ask her permission. We must do these things properly.

– Oh there's a proper way of doing everything, even screwing a goose.

But Jody, messenger of love, walks to the alcove and formally asks the lady would she drink if the gentleman at the counter sends it over. She will. She will also allow him to join her. She whispers: Has he any money?

– Loaded, says Jody.

– Send him over so. Sunday's a dull day.

Pike sits down stiffly, leaning a little away from her, which seems to her quite right for him as she has already decided that he's a shy sort of man, upperclass, but shy, not like some. He excuses himself for intruding. She says: You're not inthrudin'.

He says he hasn't the privilege of knowing her name.

Talks like a book, she decides, or a play in the Gaiety.

– Buttherfly, she says.

– Butterfly, he says, is a lovely name.

– Me mother's name was Tricksey, she volunteers.

– Was she dark like you?

– Oh, a natural blonde and very busty, well-developed you know. She danced in the old Tivoli where the newspaper office is now. I'm neat, not busty.

To his confusion she indicates, with hands moving in small curves, the parts of her that she considers are neat. But he notices that she has shapely long-fingered hands and he remembers that the poet had admitted that the small hands of his beloved were not, in fact, beautiful. He is very perturbed.

– Neat, she says, and well-made. Austin McDonnell, the fire-brigade chief, says that he read in a book that the best sizes and shapes would fit into champagne glasses.

He did wonder a little that a fire-brigade chief should be a quotable authority on female sizes and shapes, and on champagne glasses. But then and there he decides to buy her champagne, the only drink fit for such a queen who seemed as if she came, if not from China, at any rate from Japan.

– Champagne, he said.

– Bubbly, she said. I love bubbly.

Jody dusted the shoulders of the bottle that on his shelves had waited a long time for a customer. He unwired the cork. The cork and the fizz shot up to the ceiling.

– This, she said, is my lucky day.

– The divine Bernhardt, said Pike, had a bath in champagne presented to her by a group of gentlemen who admired her.

– Water, she said, is better for washing.

But she told him that her mother, who knew everything about actresses, had told her that story, and told her that when, afterwards, the gentlemen bottled the contents of the bath and drank it, they had one bottleful too many. He was too far gone in fizz and love's frenzy to feel embarrassed. She was his discovery, his oriental queen.

He said: You're very oriental in appearance. You could be from Japan.

She said: My father was, they say. A sailor. Sailors come and go.

She giggled. She said: That's a joke. Come and go. Do you see it?

Pike saw it. He giggled with her. He was a doomed man.

She said: Austin McDonnell says that if I was in Japan I could be a geisha girl if I wasn't so tall. That's why they call me Butterfly. It's the saddest story. Poor Madame Butterfly died that her child could be happy across the sea. She married a sailor, too, an American lieutenant. They come and go. The priest, her uncle, cursed her for marrying a Yank.

– The priests are good at that, said Pike who, because of his reading, allowed himself, outside office hours, a soupçon of anticlericalism.

Touched by Puccini they were silent for a while, sipping champagne. With every sip Pike realized more clearly that he had found what the poet, another poet, an English one, had called the long-awaited long-expected spring, he knew his heart had found a time to sing, the strength to soar was in his spirit's wing, that life was full of a triumphant sound and death could only be a little thing. She was good on the nose, too. She was wise in the ways of perfume. The skin of her neck had a pearly glow. The three guardian aunts were as far-away as the moon. Then one of the pub's two doors –

it was a corner house – opened with a crash and a big man came in, well drunk, very jovial. He wore a wide-brimmed grey hat. He walked to the counter. He said: Jody, old bootlegger, old friend of mine, old friend of Al Capone, serve me a drink to sober me up.

– Austin, said Jody, what will it be.

– A ball of malt, the big man said, and Madame Butterfly.

– That's my friend, Austin, she said, he always says that for a joke.

Pike whose face, with love or champagne or indignation, was taut and hot all over, said that he didn't think it was much of a joke.

– Oh, for Janey's sake, Pike, be your age.

She used his first name for the first time. His eyes were moist.

– For Janey's sake, it's a joke. He's a father to me. He knew my mother.

– He's not Japanese.

– Mind your manners. He's a fireman.

– Austin, she called. Champagne. Pike Hunter's buying champagne.

Pike bought another bottle, while Austin towered above them, swept the wide-brimmed hat from his head, in a cavalier half-circle, dropped it on the head of Jody whose red carbuncled face was thus half-extinguished. Butterfly giggled. She said: Austin, you're a scream. He knew Trixie, Pike. He knew Trixie when she was the queen of the boards in the old Tivoli.

Sitting down, the big man sang in a ringing tenor: For I knew Trixie when Trixie was a child.

He sipped at his ball of malt. He sipped at a glass of Pike's champagne. He said: It's a great day for the Irish. It's a great day to break a fiver. Butterfly, dear girl, we fixed the Longford lout. He'll never leave Longford again. The wife has him tethered and spancelled in the haggard. We wrote poison-pen letters to half the town, including the parish priest.

– I never doubted ye, she said. Leave it to the firemen, I said.

– The Dublin Fire Brigade, Austin said, has as long an arm as the Irish Republican Army.

– Austin, she told Pike, died for Ireland.

He sipped champagne. He sipped whiskey. He said: Not once, but several times. When it was neither popular nor profitable. By the living God, we was there when we was wanted. Volunteer McDonnell, at your service.

His bald head shone and showed freckles. His startlingly blue eyes were brightened and dilated by booze. He said: Did I know Trixie, light on her feet as the foam on the fountain? Come in and see the horses. That's what we used to say to the girls when I was a young fireman. Genuine horsepower the fire-engines ran on then, and the harness hung on hooks ready to drop on the horses as the firemen descended the greasy pole. And where the horses were, the hay and straw were plentiful enough to make couches for Cleopatra. That was why we asked the girls in to see the horses. The sailors from the ships, homeless men all, had no such comforts and conveniences. They used to envy us. Butterfly, my geisha girl, you should have been alive then. We'd have shown you the jumps.

Pike was affronted. He was almost prepared to say so and take the consequences. But Butterfly stole his thunder. She stood up, kissed the jovial big man smack on the bald head and then, as light on her feet as her mother ever could have been, danced up and down the floor, tight hips bouncing, fingers clicking, singing: I'm the smartest little geisha in Japan, in Japan. And the people call me Rolee Polee Nan, Polee Nan.

Drowning in desire, Pike forgot his indignation and found that he was liking the man who could provoke such an exhibition. Breathless, she sat down again, suddenly kissed Pike on the cheek, said: I love you too. I love champagne. Let's have another bottle.

They had.

A Ball of Malt and Madame Butterfly

– Rolee polee Nan, she sang as the cork and the fizz ascended.

– A great writer, a Russian, Pike said, wrote that his ideal was to be idle and to make love to a plump girl.

– The cheek of him. I'm not plump. Turkeys are plump. I love being tall, with long legs.

Displaying the agility of a trained high-kicker with hinges in her hips she, still sitting, raised her shapely right leg, up and up as if her toes would touch the ceiling, up and up until stocking-top, suspender, bare thigh and a frill of pink panties, showed. Something happened to Pike that had nothing at all to do with poetry or Jody's champagne. He held Butterfly's hand. She made a cat's cradle with their fingers and swung the locked hands pendulum-wise. She sang: Janey Mac, the child's a black, what will we do on Sunday? Put him to bed and cover his head and don't let him up until Monday.

Austin had momentarily absented himself for gentlemanly reasons. From the basement jakes his voice singing rose above the soft inland murmur of falling water: Oh my boat can lightly float in the heel of wind and weather, and outrace the smartest hooker between Galway and Kinsale.

The dockers methodically drank their pints of black porter and paid no attention. Jody said: Time's money. Why don't the two of you slip upstairs. Your heads would make a lovely pair on a pillow.

Austin was singing: Oh she's neat, oh she's sweet, she's a beauty every line, the Queen of Connemara is that bounding barque of mine.

He was so shy, Butterfly said afterwards, that he might have been a Christian Brother and a young one at that, although where or how she ever got the experience to enable her to make the comparison, or why she should think an old Christian Brother less cuthallacht than a young one, she didn't say. He told her all about the aunts and the odd way he had been reared and she, naturally, told Austin and Jody and all her sorority. But they were a kind people and no mockers, and Pike never knew, Austin told me, that Jody's clientele listened with such absorbed interest to the story of his life, and of his heart and his love-making. He was something new in their experience, and Jody's stable of girls had experienced a lot, and Austin a lot more, and Jody more than the whole shebang, and all the fire-brigade, put together.

For Jody, Austin told me, had made the price of the 'Dark Cow' in a basement in Chicago. During the prohibition, as they called it, although what they prohibited it would be hard to say. He was one of five brothers from the bogs of Manulla in the middle of nowhere in the County of Mayo. The five of them emigrated to Chicago. When Al Capone and his merry men discovered that Jody and his brethren had the real true secret about how to make the booze, and to make it good, down they went into the cellar and didn't see daylight nor breathe fresh air, except to surface to go to mass on Sundays, until they left the USA. They made a fair fortune. At least four of them did. The fifth was murdered.

Jody was a bachelor man and he was good to the girls. He took his pleasures with them as a gentleman might, with the natural result that he was poxed to the eyebrows. But he was worth more to them than the money he quite generously paid after every turn or trick on the rumpled, always un-made bed in the two-storeyed apartment above the pub. He was a kind uncle to them. He gave them a friendly welcome, a place to sit down, free drink and smokes and loans, or advances for services yet to be rendered, when they were down on their luck. He had the ear of the civic guards and could help a girl when she was in trouble. He paid fines when they were unavoidable and bills when they could no longer be postponed, and had an aunt who was reverend mother in a home for unmarried mothers and who was, like her nephew, a kindly person. Now and again, like the Madame made immortal by Maupassant, he took a bevy or flock of the girls off for a day at the seaside or in the country. A friend of mine and myself, travelling into the granite mountains south of the city, to the old stonecutters' villages of Lackan and Ballyknockan where there were aged people who had never seen Dublin, thirty miles away, and never wanted to, came upon a most delightful scene in the old country pub in Lackan. All around the bench around the walls sat the mountainy men, the stonecutters, drinking their pints. But the floor was in the possession of a score of wild girls, all dancing together, resting off and on for more drink, laughing, happy, their gaiety inspired and directed by one man in the middle of the floor: red-faced, car-buncled, oily black hair sleeked down and parted up the middle in the style of Dixie Dean, the famous soccer centre-forward, whom Jody so much admired. All the drinks were on generous Jody.

So in Jody's friendly house Pike had, as he came close to forty years, what he never had in the cold abode of the three aunts: a home, with a father, Austin, and a brother, Jody, and any God's amount of sisters; and Butterfly who, to judge by the tales she told afterwards, was a motherly sort of lover to him and, for a while, a sympathetic listener. For a while, only: because nothing in her birth, background, rearing or education, had equipped her to listen to so much poetry and talk about poetry.

— Poor Pike, she'd say, he'd puke you with poethry. Poethry's all very well, but.

She had never worked out what came after that qualifying: But.

— Give's a bar of a song, Austin. There's some sense to singing. But poethry. My heart leaps up when I behold a rainbow in the sky. On Linden when the sun was low. The Lady of Shalott left the room to go to the pot. Janey preserve us from poethry.

— He has eyes, Jody told Austin and myself, for no girl except Butterfly. Reckon, in one way, we can't blame him for that. She sure is the smartest filly showing in this paddock. But there must be moderation in all things. Big Anne, now, isn't bad, nor her sister, both well-built Mayo girls and very cooperative, nor Joany Smith from Water-

ford, nor Patty Kelly from Castleisland in the County
Kerry who married the Limey in Brum but left him when
she found he was as queer as a three-dollar-bill. And what
about little Red Mary Jones from Kilkenny City, very
attractive if it just wasn't for the teeth she lost when the
cattleman that claimed he caught gonorrhea from her gave
her an unmerciful hammering in Cumberland Street. We
got him before he left town. We cured more than his
gonorrhea.

– But, Austin said, when following your advice, Jody, and
against my own better judgement, I tried to explain all that
to Pike, what does he do but quote to me what the playboy
of the Abbey Theatre, John M. Synge, wrote in a love poem
about counting queens in Glenmacnass in the Wicklow
Mountains.

– In the Wicklow mountains, said Jody. Queens? With
the smell of the bog and the peatsmoke off them.

Austin, a great man, ever, to sing at the top of his tenor
voice about Dark Rosaleen and the Queen of Connemara
and the County of Mayo, was a literary class of a fireman.
That was one reason why Pike and himself got on so well
together, in spite of that initial momentary misunderstand-
ing about the ball of malt and Madame Butterfly.

– Seven dog-days, Austin said, the playboy said he let
pass, he and his girl, counting queens in Glenmacnass.
The queens he mentions, Jody, you never saw, even in
Chicago.

– Never saw daylight in Chicago.

– The Queen of Sheba, Austin said, and Helen, and
Maeve the warrior queen of Connacht, and Deirdre of the
Sorrows and Gloriana that was the great Elizabeth of
England and Judith out of the Bible that chopped the block
of Holofernes.

– All, said Jody, in a wet glen in Wicklow. A likely
bloody story.

– There was one queen in the poem that had an amber
belly.

– Jaundice, said Jody. Or Butterfly herself that's as

sallow as any Jap. Austin, you're a worse lunatic than Pike.

– But in the end, Jody, his own girl was the queen of all queens. They were dead and rotten. She was alive.

– Not much of a compliment to her, Jody said, to prefer her to a cartload of corpses.

– Love's love, Jody. Even the girls admit that. They've no grudge against him for seeing nobody but Butterfly.

– They give him a fool's pardon. But no doll in the hustling game, Austin, can afford to spend all her time listening to poetry. Besides, girls like a variety of pricks. Butterfly's no better or worse than the next. When Pike finds that out he'll go crazy. If he isn't crazy already.

That was the day, as I recall, that Butterfly came in wearing the fancy fur coat – just a little out of season. Jody had, for some reason or other, given her a five-pound note. Pike knew nothing about that. And Jody told her to venture the five pounds on a horse that was running at the Curragh of Kildare, that a man in Kilcullen on the edge of the Curragh had told him that the jockey's wife had already bought her balldress for the victory celebration. The Kilcullen man knew his onions, and his jockeys, and shared his wisdom only with a select few so as to keep the odds at a good twenty to one.

– She's gone out to the bookie's, said Jody, to pick up her winnings. We'll have a party tonight.

Jody had a tenner on the beast.

– She could invest it, said Austin, if she was wise. The day will come when her looks will go.

– Pike might propose to her, said Jody. He's mad enough for anything.

– The aunts would devour him. And her.

– Here she comes, Jody said. She invested her winnings on her fancy back.

She had too, and well she carried them in the shape of pale or silver musquash, and three of her sorority walked behind her like ladies-in-waiting behind the queen of England. There was a party in which even the dockers

joined, but not Pike, for that evening and night one of the
aunts was at death's door in a nursing-home, and Pike and
the other two aunts were by her side. He wasn't to see that
musquash until he took Butterfly on an outing to the
romantic hill of Howth where the poet and the woman had
seen the white birds. That was the last day Pike ever took
Butterfly anywhere. The aunt recovered. They were a
thrawn hardy trio.

Pike had become a devotee. Every day except Sunday he
lunched in Jody's, on a sandwich of stale bread and leathery
ham and a glass of beer, just on the off chance that Butterfly
might be out of the doss and abroad, and in Jody's, at that,
to her, unseasonable hour of the day. She seldom was, except when she was deplorably short of money. In the better
eating-places on Grafton Street and Stephen's Green, his
colleagues absorbed the meals that enabled higher civil
servants to face up to the afternoon and the responsibilities
of State: statistics, land commission, local government,
finance, posts and telegraphs, internal revenue. He had
never, among his own kind, been much of a mixer: so that
few of his peers even noticed the speed with which, when at
five in the evening the official day was done, he took himself,
and his hat and coat and umbrella, and legged it off to
Jody's: in the hope that Butterfly might be there, bathed
and perfumed and ready for wine and love. Sometimes she
was. Sometimes she wasn't. She liked Pike. She didn't deny
it. She was always an honest girl, as her mother, Tricksey,
had been before her – so Austin said when he remembered
Tricksey who had died in a hurry, of peritonitis. But, Janey
Mac, Butterfly couldn't have Pike Hunter for breakfast,
dinner, tea and supper, and nibblers as well, all the livelong
day and night. She still, as Jody said, had her first million to
make, and Pike's inordinate attachment was coming between her and the real big business, as when, say, the
country cattle men were in town for the market. They were
the men who knew how to get rid of the money.

– There is this big cattleman, she tells Austin once, big

he is in every way, who never knows or cares what he's spending. He's a gift and a godsend to the girls. He gets so drunk that all you have to do to humour him is play with him a little in the taxi going from pub to pub and see that he gets safely to his hotel. The taximen are on to the game and get their divvy out of the loot.

One wet and windy night, it seems, Butterfly and this philanthropist are flying high together, he on brandy, she on champagne, for which that first encounter with Pike has given her a ferocious drouth. In the back of the taxi, touring from pub to pub, the five-pound notes are flowing out of your man like water out of a pressed sponge. Butterfly is picking them up and stuffing them into her handbag, but not all of them. For this is too good and too big for any taximan on a fair percentage basis. So for every one note she puts into her handbag she stuffs two or three down into the calf-length boots she is wearing against the wet weather. She knows, you see, that she is too far gone in bubbly to walk up the stairs to her own room, that the taximan, decent fellow, will help her up and then, fair enough, go through her bag, and take his cut. Which, indeed, in due time he does. When she wakes up, fully clothed, in the morning on her own bed, and pulls off her boots, her ankles, what with the rain that had dribbled down into her boots, are poulticed and plastered with notes of the banks of Ireland and of England, and one moreover of the Bank of Bonnie Scotland.

– Rings on my fingers, she says, and bells on my toes.

That was the gallant life that Pike's constant attendance was cutting her off from. She also hated being owned. She hated other people thinking that she was owned. She hated like hell when Pike would enter the 'Dark Cow' and one of the other girls, or, worse still, another man, a bit of variety, would move away from her side to let Pike take the throne. They weren't married, for Janey's sake. She could have hated Pike, except that she was as tender-hearted as Trixie had been, and she liked champagne. She certainly felt at liberty to hate the three aunts who had made a molly coddle out of

him. She also hated, with a hatred that grew and grew, the
way that Pike puked her with poethry. And all this time
poor Pike walked in a dream that he never defined for us,
perhaps not even for himself, but that certainly must have
looked higher than the occasional trick on Jody's rumpled
bed. So dreaming, sleep-walking, he persuaded Butterfly
to go to Howth Head with him one dull hot day when the
town was empty and she had nothing better to do. No
place could have been more fatally poetic than Howth. She
wore her musquash. Not even the heat could part her from
it.

– He never let up, she said, not once from the moment
we boarded the bus on the quays. Poethry. I had my belly-
ful.

– Sure thing, said Jody.

– Any man, she said, that won't pay every time he per-
forms is a man to keep a cautious eye on. Not that he's not
generous. But at the wrong times. Money down or no play's
my motto.

– Well I know that, Jody said.

– But Pike Hunter says that would make our love mercenary, whatever that is.

– You're a great girl, said Austin, to be able to pronounce
it.

– Your middle name, said Jody, is mercenary.

– My middle name, thank you, is Imelda. And the cheek
of Pike Hunter suggesting to me to go to a doctor because he
noticed something wrong with himself, a kidney disorder, he
said. He must wet the bed.

– Butterfly, said Austin, he might have been giving you
good advice.

– Nevertheless. It's not for him to say.

When they saw from the bus the Bull Wall holding the
northern sand back from clogging up the harbour, and the
Bull Island, three miles long, with dunes, bent grass, golfers,
bathers and skylarks, Pike told her about some fellow called
Joyce – there was a Joyce in the Civic Guards, a Galwayman
who played county football, but no relation – who had

gone walking on the Island one fine day and laid eyes on a young one, wading in a pool, with her skirts well pulled up; and let a roar out of him. By all accounts this Joyce was no addition to the family for, as Pike told the story, Butterfly worked out that the young one was well under age.

Pike and Butterfly had lunch by the edge of the sea, in the Clairmont Hotel, and that was all right. Then they walked in the grounds of Howth Castle, Pike had a special pass and the flowers and shrubs were a sight to see if only Pike had kept his mouth shut about some limey by the name of Spenser who had landed there in the year of God and wrote a poem as long as from here to Killarney about a fairy queen and a gentle knight who was pricking on the plain like the members of the Harp Cycling Club, Junior Branch, up above there in the Phoenix Park. He didn't get time to finish the poem (the poet that is, not Pike), for the Cork people burned him out of house and home and, as far as Butterfly was concerned, that was the only good deed she ever heard attributed to the Cork people.

The Phoenix Park and the Harp Club reminded her that one day Jody had said, meaning no harm, about the way Pike moped around the 'Dark Cow' when Butterfly wasn't there, that Pike was the victim of a semi-horn and should go up to the Fifteen Acres in the Park and put it in the grass for a while and run around it. But when, for fun, she told this to Pike he got so huffed he didn't speak for half an hour, and they walked Howth Head until her feet were blistered and the heel of her right shoe broke, and the sweat, with the weight of the musquash and the heat of the day, was running between her shoulder blades like a cloud-burst down the gutter. Then the row and the ructions, as the song says, soon began. He said she should have worn flatheeled shoes. She said that if she had known that he was conscripting her for a forced march over a mountain she'd have borrowed a pair of boots from the last soldier she gave it to at cut-price, for the soldiers, God help them, didn't have much money but they were more openhanded with what they had than some people who had plenty, and soldiers didn't waste time and breath on poetry: Be you fat or be you lean there is no soap like Preservene.

So she sat on the summit of Howth and looked at the lighthouse and the seagulls, while Pike walked back to the village to have the broken heel mended, and the sweat dried cold on her, and she was perished. Then when he came back, off he was again about how that whiteheaded old character that you'd see across the river there at the Abbey Theatre, and Madame Gone Mad MacBride that was the age of ninety and looked it, and known to all as a roaring rebel, worse than Austin, had stood there on that very spot, and how the poet wrote a poem wishing for himself and herself to be turned into seagulls, the big dirty brutes that you'd see along the docks robbing the pigeons of their food. Butterfly would have laughed at him, except that her teeth by this time were tap-dancing with the cold like the twinkling feet of Fred Astaire. So she pulled her coat around her and said: Pike, I'm no seagull. For Janey's sake take me back to civilization and Jody's where I know someone.

But, God sees, you never knew nobody, for at that moment the caveman came out in Pike Hunter, he that was always so backward on Jody's bed and, there and then, he tried to flatten her in the heather in full view of all Dublin and the coast of Ireland as far south as Wicklow Head and as far north as where the Mountains of Mourne sweep down to the sea.

– Oh none of that, Pike Hunter, she says, my good musquash will be crucified. There's a time and a place and a price for everything.

– You and your musquash, he tells her.

They were wrestling like Man Mountain Dean and Jack Doyle, the Gorgeous Gael.

– You've neither sense nor taste, says he, to be wearing a fur coat on a day like this.

– Bloody well for you to talk, says she, with your rolled umbrella and your woollen combinations and your wobbly ass that won't keep you straight in the chair, and your three witches of maiden aunts never touched, tasted or handled by mortal man, and plenty of money and everything your own way. This is my only coat that's decent, in case you haven't noticed, and I earned it hard and honest with Jody, a generous man but a monster on the bed, I bled after him.

That put a stop to the wrestling. He brought her back to the 'Dark Cow' and left her at the door and went his way.

He never came back to the 'Dark Cow' but once, and Butterfly wasn't on her throne that night. It was the night before the cattle-market. He was so lugubrious and woebegone that Jody and Austin and a few merry newspapermen including myself tried to jolly him up, take him out of himself, by making jokes at his expense that would force him to come alive and answer back. Our efforts failed. He looked at us sadly and said: Boys, Beethoven, when he was dying, said: Clap now, good friends, the comedy is done.

He was more than a little drunk and for the first time, seemed lopsided when standing up; and untidy.

– Clap now indeed, said Jody.

Pike departed and never returned. He took to steady drinking in places like the Shelbourne Hotel or the Buttery in the 'Hibernian' where it was most unlikely, even with Dublin being the democratic sort of town that it is, that he would ever encounter Madame Butterfly. He became a great problem for his colleagues and his superior officers in the civil service, and for his three aunts. After careful consultation they, all together, persuaded him to rest up in St Patrick's Hospital where, as you all may remember, Dean Swift died roaring. Which was, I feel sure, why Pike wasn't there to pay the last respects to the dead when Jody dropped from a heart attack and was waked in the bedroom above the 'Dark Cow'. The girls were there in force to say an eternal farewell to a good friend. Since the drink was plentiful and the fun and the mourning intense, somebody, not even Austin knew who, suggested that the part of the corpse that the girls knew best should be tastefully decorated with black crêpe ribbon. The honour of tying on the ribbon naturally went to Madame Butterfly but it was Big Anne who burst into tears and cried out: Jody's dead and gone forever.

Austin met her, Butterfly not Big Anne, a few days afterwards at the foot of the Nelson Pillar. Jody's successor had routed the girls from the 'Dark Cow'. Austin told her about Pike and where he was. She brooded a bit. She said it was a pity, but nobody could do nothing for him, that those three aunts had spoiled him forever and, anyway, didn't Austin think that he was a bit astray in the head.

– Who knows, Butterfly? Who's sound or who's silly? Consider yourself for a moment.

– What about me, Austin?

– A lovely girl like you, a vision from the romantic east, and think of the life you lead. It can have no good ending. Let me tell you a story, Butterfly. There was a girl once in London, a slavey, a poor domestic servant. I knew a redcoat here in the old British days who said he preferred slaveys to anything else because they were clean, free and flattering.

– Austin, I was never a slavey.

– No Butterfly, you have your proper pride. But listen: this slavey is out one morning scrubbing the stone steps in front of the big house she works in, bucket and brush, carbolic soap and all that, in one of the great squares in one of the more classy parts of London Town. There she is on her bended knees when a gentleman walks past, a British army major in the Coldstream Guards or the Black Watch or something.

– I've heard of them, Austin.

– So this British major looks at her and he sees the naked backs of her legs, thighs you know, and he taps her on the shoulder or somewhere and he says: oh, rise up, lovely maiden and come along with me, there's a better life in store for you somewhere else. She left the bucket and the brush, and the stone steps half-scrubbed, and walked off with him and became his girl. But there were even greater things in store for her. For Butterfly, that slavey became

Lady Emma Hamilton, the beloved of Lord Nelson, the greatest British sailor that ever sailed, and the victor at the renowned battle of Trafalgar. There he is up on the top of the Pillar.

– You wouldn't think to look at him, Austin, that he had much love in him.

– But, Butterfly, meditate on that story, and rise up, and get yourself out of the gutter. You're handsome enough to be the second Lady Hamilton.

After that remark, Austin brought her into 'Lloyd's', a famous house of worship in North Earl Street under the shadow of Lord Nelson and his pillar. In 'Lloyd's' he bought her a drink and out of the kindness of his great singing heart, gave her some money. She shook his hand and said: Austin, you're the nicest man I ever met.

Austin had, we may suppose, given her an image, an ideal. She may have been wearied by Pike and his sad attachment to poetry, but she rose to the glimmering vision of herself as a great lady beloved by a great and valiant lord. A year later she married a docker, a decent quiet hardworking fellow who had slowly sipped his pints of black porter and watched and waited all the time.

– Oddly enough, Austin told me when the dignity of old age had gathered around him like the glow of corn-stubble in the afterwards of harvest.

He could still sing. His voice never grew old.

– Oddly enough, I never had anything to do with her. That way, I mean. Well, you know me. Fine wife, splendid sons, nobody like them in the world. Fine daughters, too. But a cousin of mine, a ship's wireless operator who had been all round the world from Yokohama to the Belgian Congo and back again, and had had a ship burned under him in Bermuda and, for good value, another ship burned under him in Belfast, said she was the meanest whore he ever met. When he had paid her the stated price, there were some coppers left in his hand and she grabbed them and said give us these for the gas-meter. But he said, also, that at the high moments she had a curious and diverting way of raising and bending and extending her left leg – not her right leg which she kept as flat as a plumb-level. He had never encountered the like before, in any colour or in any country.

Andrew Travers

Babyface

Alone.

I shove the Yale key into my wife's front door and the oiled way it runs in to the hilt and the vicious way I turn it remind me of me in her (the door opens and in my memory I roll off her to sleep while she stares on at the ceiling).

The torso of noise of a taxi outside grows an arm which reaches into the hall and grows fingers which index through my mind until I close the door. The crunch of the closing door uses its life to run into the kitchen, and dies tripping a switch in my wife. Me and my reflection cast our coats at either side of the hall mirror and in the other world she thinks I live in my weight doubles as I absorb her reflection, standing next to mine.

(I want to turn in my body to her away from my clutching flesh, but I am my own cannibal.)

Dry winds of boredom blow about clouding me. Smile, question, interest, rejection, hatred: she tries to grasp my expression which arrives in stages like a row of fruits in a fruit-machine. Nothing.

(I tell her the truth about herself, as I understand it, she listens but does not believe it. We have a row with knives and scalding coffee [poisonous words, despair and separation]. The city [it seems a coagulation of people and machines which walks through time] has chosen this future from the alternatives for a mouthful of its evening meal.)

([If I could reach out, into the future. Grow arms and hands from my torso past, strangle my future self in the act of turning me as if I was a walking doll and placing an axe in my hand as I advance in a new direction towards her instead of him.])

Using our silence as receptacle the city diarrhoeas the ringing of the phone.

('You can't bat in that league.' My father's phrase about his first rich wife teleprints itself in time with the STD pips in Janet's ear [Y-pip, O-pip, U-pip . . . pippippippip – AGUE] as the caller fumbles a sixpence into the vandals' welfare box across the blank paper of all those letters I have yet to write to her from other miseries; [my father contracting his first marriage to a cricket match with a phrase] – the players [he and his wife] becoming me and Janet-on-the-phone. [I have been bowling from the gasometer end all evening and no wickets have fallen.] The caller gets his sixpence in and [like through a fruit-machine] his voice passes through Janet's brain, 'Peter darling!' Janet's voice soars high over my grandstand where I spectate my destruction. A six. 'Tomorrow evening. Lovely.' Another six. She places the receiver on the hook. I clap. 'What are you clapping for?' she asks in the voice she uses when I have one of my mock epileptic fits. 'Because you have had a good innings.' She becomes a human question mark. I leave the room and two rooms away baring my teeth at my reflection in the bathroom mirror can almost feel her shrug her shoulders.)

I look at the mirror. You stupid creature. I laugh. My reflection does not flinch. I cry. Why can't you kill yourself. My reflection does not flinch. I laugh. Then my reflection looks at me. We laugh, we do not cry.

([8.53 p.m. I am in the grip of an anger as difficult to disperse as the bathroom around me, the building around it, and the city around the building. I wash my hands in the sink. I pull out the plug, and as slowly and as deviously as that water travelling through sewers to the Thames and the North Sea I trickle out of my anger into as large a despair via memories (half involuntary and half revived by a most strenuous exertion of my will) of how Janet and I used to be. 8.58 p.m.])

(The feeling of being hunted by Janet; as if by hurting me she can make me say obviously untrue words like 'You are ugly' so that she can skin me of them and demonstrate that there is nothing I can ever say about her again which will protect me.)

(The other feeling that anybody would be more brutal in describing my feelings than Janet in creating them in me.)

([They would have said, 'He is in a bad mood.' I could have said, 'A bad mood is in me.' I am dissolving in a bad mood, a bad mood is dissolving in me.])

(I look through the bathroom keyhole at Janet washing. It reminds me of looking at her when she is asleep through the keyhole of my consciousness when she is washed in her dreams.)

I love my wife but she does not love me; I hate her. (My wife hates me.)

(As I clean my teeth – foaming at the mouth – I hear Janet in the kitchen entangled in clattering noises. Eight years of clattering to make a mountain of sound tunnelled by conversations from 'I love you' at one side to 'I hate you' at the other. The broken crockery and smashed mirrors are avalanches on this mountain. I try to reach the summit with a rope of words and all that's there is silence.)

I have been minced (married) eight years – Strindberg bouillabaisse.

(As I switch off the bedroom light she says she won't be back tomorrow night.)

Once again my ruthless unremitting honesty has lost me a wife. (*That* joke.)

(11.35 p.m. I turn the Yale key in the front door, more getting out of outside than getting into inside. In the hall I am alone. The memory of her standing next to me the day before as I take off my coat facing the hall mirror sinks in me as I free my arms. I am a struggling man-fly in a cloud of droplet seconds [time's aerosol spray].)

(I turn on the gas under the full kettle and inhale before lighting it. The gasman *malgré-lui*. It soaks my memory in suicide. Perfectly, I make a cup of tea. I drink it without thirst in the bedroom, my ears cocked to pick up her key in the front door. I sniff a pair of her pants trapped beneath a bed leg. Strident. While I am on all fours I switch on the electric blanket. I feel like an apartment cat. I pounce on the bed. I sleep. She is standing over me sneering. I think, 'Run for your life.' She thinks, 'And that heap of graceless ugly bad-tempered petulant insufferable flesh apparently intends to share my bed.' [That is what she is to say.])

(If I had had a diary where I had written she was a bitch and she had read it it would explain her face.)

(The next five minutes are a snowstorm, to be fought through, blind and freezing.)

([She runs at me with a breadknife. I dodge and bash her head with my closed fist as it passes me. She lays herself on the floor in her crying position.])

Her left thigh is bare on the lino. It is grey, it is cold to the touch. Stone. Statuesque.

(I am talking to her again.)

([My words must arrive in her like a row of fruits in a fruit-machine. Though she never scoops up any of the prizes (my meanings). As for the Mystery Jackpot, ('You make me sick') perhaps walking down a street one day she will experience a collapse of her thoughts in a profusion of emotions.])

Two years later I am walking eastwards down the Embankment; a black Jaguar passes me, two uniformed policemen in the front and a Detective Constable in the back examine me with the aid of a combined IQ of 301 and 16 O-Levels. I am glad I did not murder Janet. She will be snoring now. If she has been crying black trickles will have dried from her eyes to her jawline, very fine black hair packing her head into a blue pillow like a half-unwrapped birthday present of a glazed bowl in a nightmare. (This nightmare.) (Across the Thames Battersea Power Station like a profane cathedral worships the city with electricity.) (By the light of a sodium lamp-post I read my watch.)

1.49 a.m. I realize I have been passing through the city to the room of a girl I worked with at the bank whom I had promised to phone earlier.

As I proceed to her room (despising myself) I quote to myself a summary of the speech that had won her sympathy. 'At thirty-three,' (I age another twelve years, advance into a book-heavy study [because of these pedantic words] on middle-age creep, paunch and resignation first, dragging this thirty-three year old behind them, but who does not need dragging because he runs into the forty-five year old biographer eagerly with the words 'At thirty-three . . .'), 'I am too old to do what I want and old enough to not want to, I am young enough to feel old and old enough to feel young. I am bored to death.' She swallowed it. And so do I.

(Tick tick tick like a sixpence in a fruit-machine.) (Down the steps.) Other basement steps pass upwards under me in my memory as I descend. She is in. One of *these* days she will be out. Or an unpleasant person will be with her. As I reach the bottom step a suspicion hares in the other direction up the mental stairs which run from love to hate – *too* pleased. (But in I grin already saying other words than I had planned, chasing after qualifications and subordinate clauses, interrupting myself, sitting down, standing up, lighting a cigarette, drinking a cup of tea). In chaos. As in other basements.

(Her lavatory over-fascinates me. I suspect it is an echo-chamber so I never shit in it. Besides, making a smell seems the surest way to render myself physically uncommunicable. She hasn't used much toilet tissue since Thursday. Constipation?) (Too late, I am having the father and mother of a shit. My food passes slowly through me and then through the sewers into the Thames and the North Sea. And in the dimension of time I am being forced down a long thin intestine in the giant transparent amoeba of the city.)

She likes to put a record on, make two cups of tea and sit with me smoking cigarettes on the rug in front of the gasfire.

It would be perfect for anyone but me. The record revolves and while the needle curves for the centre I'm spun outwards through my memories from her room (us) because looking at her face not seeing the face I want to see not allowing myself to look away I begin to separate from my expression like a solid from a liquid in a centrifuge (myself hardening into my solidifying past in the whirl of time beneath a liquid present [my fluent smile] which evaporates into the future . . .).

She is beside me. I look at the two hillocks of her breasts forming the letter B. They are volcanoes waiting to erupt milk, about to burst, – busts. 'He was beside himself.'

I push my penis into her cunt, move it about gently for a few minutes, and she comes; out of a chrysalis of moans and heavy breathing she hatches on the bed, emerging from a cocoon of endearments like a glistening adult-size baby, stranded on her back. Like a mother severing the umbilical cord I pull out my penis.

(Wearing fur boiler-suits her two nude cats gallop in. They roll on the rug in front of the fire biting and scratching. Then they lie still.)

When I come in her my skin becomes a mould and frees a diving (diminishing) replica inside which swims into her, and inflates to fill her exactly as she places her lips on mine – I kiss myself. How do you do. (Fuck you.) Momentarily I have fallen unrequitedly in love with myself.

I press and bulge her face with my bitten-nail fingers, sexlessly, like a sculptor whose clay has turned to rubber. When it occurs to her I am behaving like a madman she says, 'You're hurting me.' I want to slash her.

She looks to me like a petite dark girl whose orgasm has distended her in several ways – her legs beneath the sheet are fatter, her exposed breasts are larger and more sagging with coarser nipples, her teeth protrude more, her lips are more generous, and her dark brown eyes have gone pale blue while her short black hair has stretched and bleached long and blonde. I prefer the pre-orgasm version, the girl I am in bed with is not BB.

(I sleep. When I wake I decide to have a day off work. [I am a shop assistant, I was fired from the bank over a year ago.] 'Downward social mobility' – the personnel officer, trained in sociology, wrote on my form.)

Towards the end of the Jimmy Young programme I hear voices through the lime emulsioned wall. A man repeatedly shouts, 'But I haven't got any more money,' and his wife repeatedly screams 'Will you shut up.' After half an hour the wife misses an 'up' and stops. 'Will you shut up, will you shut up, will you shut – ' I imagine a razor across the throat and then instead a breadknife between the shoulders.

The afternoon imprisons me as much as the room.

(The revving of a lorry drives through the room dragging its load of noise through a thousand furnished rooms.)

I leave the house where I had slept; in the air I try to wrench backwards from my walking figure; (inside me the seed of a future self who will interpret my progress down the street with the phrase 'He walked mechanically'). I want to go home to Janet, as she had been, but can't because she isn't like that now, but I am like I was, only more so. Realizing that is like being sentenced to thirty years or as if instead of saying 'I love you' someone I love says 'I do not love you'. But I can still touch the underside of the words I need to inhabit (like a man springing in the trampyline of his thoughts making a last great effort) before those words fly into the past behind me (like the reflection one has of oneself in the mirror burying in her because at one's shoulder one's unloving wife appears and one unthinking smiles at her reflection), those words weighting the gramophone needle of my body on the record of my world, 'I love you', without which I slide across and scar faces I see but don't absorb. (I can rotate succeeding faces but hers does not surface, or run my fingers to the nose and from laugh lines pick up cries.) Her absence is like the absence of an amputated arm when its nerves delineate it with pains. Walking down the street those nerves of absence reach into my future from which I try to cut myself with the hacksawing edges of words. I try to lag behind myself.

... a man skids to a halt wearing a Ford van. He comes to the door. With road-devouring eyes my father drives through me to my mother in the kitchen ...

... in my parents' house I stand at my bedroom window; aged five, seventeen, twenty-five, thirty-three.... In the back garden adjoining ours is a football game between in-laws and the children. Thud, smack, crash. Thud, smack, crash. (The waltz of worry, *circa* 1960.) A lawnmower in the distance, up and down, up and down, stitches this morning in my memory to all the other identical mornings, an aural patchwork blanket tucked over my mind before sleep; thirty-three, fifty, seventy-five ...

... at mealtimes my parents try to worm out of me where I got my money from to pay them for my keep. (The money I took from the till at the butcher's shop where I worked.) Like themselves the food my parents eat is either greasy or sweet ...

... a group from Los Angeles is being interviewed on the radio. Their new record is 'Truck Driving Blues'. 'Did any of you ever drive a truck?' asks the interviewer. A pained voice replies, 'No, I drive a Porsche.' I drive myself, I think. Up through the gears, round the corners, into a brick wall ....

... because I do not work and do not want to my parents arranged for me to see a psychiatrist. He told me to regard what I had been feeling for the last two years as an illness. As he spoke of cure, as though Janet were a cancer, and adjustment, as though I were an instrument or machine, I could not help the retort, '*Your* health is the real illness.' He said nothing after that, but prescribed some pills (which will pass through me like sixpences etc. .... Nothing). I imagine meeting him in the street. I say, 'You make me sick,' and leave him standing speechless. Really he is an intelligent fool. But he wears the white coat and he has the qualifications. Next time I see him I will frighten him with a story, describe how I broke into the room of a girl I used to know, strangled her two cats, put them in her bed side by side like children, with a ribbon round each of their necks ...

It is Saturday lunchtime in a pub in Kensington. I am
drinking a light ale with a friend from Out-Patients (we
met waiting through Thursday afternoons). A girl he knows
wends through the other customers towards us, as I study
her the following dialogue between her and her husband I
imagine she might have just had wends through my mind.
What are you looking at me like that for? I'm not looking at you
like anything. *Why are you so angry?* What have I said that
could make you think I am angry. *It's not what you said it's
the way you said it.* You're imagining it, you're inventing it to
make me angry. *Now you are angry!* If I'm angry only now
how could I have been angry before? *There's been nothing in
what I've said to make you angry as you are now, so you must
have been cross with me before.* Cross! Cross! What are you
talking about, I'm just sitting here trying to read the paper
. . . (she bumps into a fat man drinking a pint of beer) . . .
*'Just sitting here trying to read the paper', what was stopping you?
In any case you weren't trying to read the paper, all I could hear was
flick flick flick, crackle, crackle, crackle; and heavy breathing and
grunting, and those looks you were giving me* – Well, you've got
what you wanted. Saturday morning, the whole weekend
to get through, and us both shouting at each other already.
Is that what you wanted? . . . (she brushes against a lined
woman in rabbit drinking Guinness) . . . *You suffocate me.* I
should. *Yes, that's what you'd really like to do isn't it?* No, I just
want to read the paper. *Alright, I won't interfere with your
reading pleasure any more, I'm going out.* Go, and don't come
back, you make me sick. *One of these days I won't.* That would
be better than you coming back in the middle of Saturday
night stinking of gin . . . (she collides with an old age pen-
sioner who spills half of his half-pint) . . . *Believe me, I
wouldn't drink if I didn't need to. Living with you it's the only way
to get relief.* You mean, living with yourself. *I'm going, enjoy
your paper darling.* (I can go no further [she is saying hello to
me] because I am losing track of who is saying what. The
next round is on me; she asks for gin.)

(She has to go shopping. We arrange to call on her at
seven. By then my friend has disappeared. 'Acting out of

character' because I am so lonely I take a taxi to her address.)

I press with the third finger of my left hand the bell that armour-pierces the silence of her house, recoiling back from the tip of that finger at the same rate as the bell drills through her, until almost wholly drowned in my body I do a swimmer's somersault-turn at the shallow end of myself, and with a different tiredness (of her now, not of myself) I plough forward by expressing nothing with my face face to face with her face through a six-inch opened door, she does not admit me.

(October: sky the colour of raw liver. Meat world. I am eating the view from the ward window.)

(November: fat dark grey clouds just above the trees roll west, looking up is like looking down from a light plane losing height in an Atlantic storm.)

(December: the snowfall on the branches has settled like talcum powder on pubic hair. [The body is Hertford-shire.])

([March: I write to Janet. 'Since October I have been in this mental hospital. I have attempted suicide twice. I have made three wastepaper baskets and a rug. There were days which lasted for ever. And you slowly went away.'])

(Janet faces me in the dayroom. She has slipped off her new fur coat. We hear the complex tinklings of teacups on a trolley along a corridor. About to sip her tea she says, 'Che today. Gone tomorrow.' [My pillar of weakness, lengthen-ing.])

I have been lethargic so they have given me ametha-mines. I can face watching T V with the others now. The news. Czechoslovakia, Biafra, Asia ... like brides nobody's humanity would marry the words file past our ears, puffed out by their final As; 'a', 'ah', 'Aaah!' Like sixpences through fruit-machines; nothing, nothing, nothing. But then, 'I ought to care.' I think, if this is marriage, and there is an offspring, if it's a girl I'll call it – ('No!' – It is a man trying to explain that he does not want Electro-Convulsive

Therapy before the male nurse gives him his general anaesthetic) – and if it's a boy – ('No!' – The needle sinks into his vein) – *Bolivery* ... (Bolivia? Bovary? Ovary? ...)

(The psychiatrist is telling me that I may leave the hospital. He asks, 'Do you feel better?' As I listen behind my vandal mask to my reply I say to myself 'You know they're not interested yet you trot out your little answer, anxious to please, begging for their attention.' If I was someone else I would continue, 'You make me sick.' And I would leave the room.)

Release. I don't know what to do with myself. My physical presence is a stumbling block between myself as I don't want to be and myself as I want to be.

Walking down the drive out of the hospital I am not alone. My companion says he is happy. If I were him I would be unhappy. If he were me he would be happier. I am unhappy.

(I pass out of the hospital, eyed [savaged] by the porter at the gate. In a park's bushes I remove my trousers and underpants. A plainclothes policewoman sits on a bench in front of where I hide. 'Hello,' I call. As she turns towards me I open my mac. I look down at myself [Janet called me 'Pig']. The policewoman screams. I wanted to say, 'Look what has been done to me,' and all they can say is, 'Look what he does to us.' Suicide. Once again the word bacon-slices through me, the cutting edge of her scream.)

Andrew Travers

Don't Shoot

I, I, I, I, – Mississippi . . .

I will have only myself to turn to – that fucking maniac.

Six hours: through blue sky, through bluer sky, through clouds, a long straight white vapour trail at fifty thousand feet will connect Kennedy and Heathrow.

I will be looking at, following the *weave* of my jeans, the interesting patterns the creases behind my left knee will make of it. It will be a change from the Atlantic Ocean. I will look out of the porthole on my right and Slough (Slo-ugh, ugh, 'Ugh!') will appear from under the right wing, napalmed by the Boeing's roar.

The male passenger on my left will (aurally digested by me) finish his banana. I will compare him to a defective automat fruit dispenser in reverse. I will say to myself to amuse myself, 'Bashing them in the right spot can make them work better.' Then he will be sick into a brown paper bag.

Across the aisle an old female Texan will be smoking a cigarette and turning the pages of Life magazine and sipping a martini – it will be like watching a bad juggler, I will have to look away. She will drop her smile.

I will like a feeling. I will dislike a feeling. Like. Dislike. Like. Dislike. Dislike. Etc.

Heathrow Airport pasted on to the rest of England will rise to meet me in my Boeing to give me a rubber bump up my spine. Map!

I will be in a panic; an extrapolation at this instant of

some of my thoughts into words – by forces beyond my control – would become new orders to the pilot, 'More throttle, you cannot land here, take off – ' but the conveyor belt I will have stepped on to at Kennedy will seem bound to deposit me in the dock of Uxbridge Magistrates Court, charged with Possessing a Firearm and Illegal Entry.

'Not guilty, not guilty, not guilty – ' they will not believe me, they will not listen, I will be a lump blocking his view of the air hostess, like a comedian on T V with the volume off gobbling air . . . What I will be saying will be 'Could you pass my case?' to the banana man who will have been sitting it out until all the other passengers have disembarked, he will be having a sign conversation with the air hostess and I will have left my case under my seat.

'Aliens.' I will say it to myself to amuse myself.

I will have travelled on British, Canadian, Swedish and American passports and will feel richest handing over an American passport. It will say I am a film director. The Customs Officer will give it back with a silent very good sir. To buck myself up I will say to myself, 'Keep sucking sucker!'

I will go to the Gents, change a dollar with the attendant who will take his 20 per cent, drop sixpence in a slot and have an electric shave (the mirror will have been smashed) by touch. I will look in the mirror over the sinks and *somehow* will not have expected to see my face there, so familiar, so strange, in such a familiar, such a strange place.

I will like a feeling. I will dislike a feeling. I will not be able to bear a feeling. Etc.

Talgarth Road, West Cromwell Road, Cromwell Road. W.14 becoming S.W.5. Three lanes of traffic five or six vehicles deep moving from red light to red light. What I will feel? What I will think? What I will say? In that order?

I will check into an Earls Court hotel, sign the register with another name and carrying my case follow the receptionist to the second floor and along a corridor to room 28. The receptionist will open the door, stand aside for me to

enter and wait until sure I have no immediate requests.
Zero. When the receptionist will have gone I will close the
door, place my case on the bed and drop the key onto a
glass topped bedside table where it (the key, the plastic disc
with 28 on it, the ring coupling key to disc) will come to rest
in an irregular arrangement with the final sound of a ball
in a roulette wheel on an unbacked number, (metal and
plastic on glass), like a miniaturized clank of a freight wagon
halted by buffers.

In the sink will be a squeezed out tube of toothpaste with
no cap. I will say to myself to amuse myself, 'The previous
occupant had teeth.'

The square of dusty newspaper at the bottom of the wastepaper bin where I will throw the used tube will give an
account (written by a likeable young man with a promising
career) of the trial of a doctor accused of indecently
assaulting a nine-year-old girl patient.

I feel sorry for you I will say to myself.

I will look under the bed to nail any verminous hopes
that might have been trying to live off me. A tampax, a wire
coat-hanger, five cigarette ends, a left gymshoe. All my life
people will have been telling me, 'Wipe that smile off your
face.' Now it will be their things which will do that.

I will have a wash and when I pull out the plug the water
will stay where it was. Grey, luke, sullen. The water will
stay where it was when I pull out the plug.

I will not be able to bear a feeling. I will not be able to
bear a feeling. I will not be able to bear a feeling. Etc. On
the surface of my mind, a speck of scum, will be the phrase,
'The turning point of my life.'

The water will very slowly (grey, luke, sullen, luke, grey)
revolve in the sink.

It will be as obvious I had no control over this, (it will be
larger, hairier, a slightly different shape [I will be looking at
my naked – 'Don't shoot!' – body in a mirror] than it used
to be) as that what I will have done and will do is also beyond my control.

I will look out of the window of my hotel room and a

Mercedes will draw up at the other side of the road. A Korean in Levis and a girl in a PVC jacket will get out? He will hit her across the face. They will get back in and the car will drive off.

A muddy Volkswagen will stop in front of the hotel. I will compare it to a metal octopus with human arms and legs as it discharges some muscular male and female New Zealanders from its front and rear doors – they will enter the foyer below me, their normal voices will pour into my room through the window and also up the stairs along the corridor and under the door.

I will draw the curtains, lay on the bed.

I will think, 'I would have survived had it not been for that ceiling.' Though it will be a normal hotel room ceiling with darkening flaking emulsion, cracks and several maps of Cuba and Vietnam where heavy feet above will have loosened the plaster I will know that this is what will have been there always above me if I looked up. It will be the true lid on my life.

I will think, 'There are pills to combat this.' I will swallow two nembutal and six aspirin, bloom, and I will go to bed without undressing.

I will dream I land slowly on the hotel room's ceiling which will be the moon's surface. My footprints, just two of them, one like Cuba, the other Vietnam. A voice shouting, 'Cuba, Vietnam. Cuba, Vietnam – ' modulates into a sergeant's, 'Left, right. Left, right – ' and I will be one of a huge platoon marching across a flat land. When I will wake dozens of Lilliputian New Zealanders will be dancing on my 12 ft by 10 ft forehead. (Someone will fall against my door and in the same split-second I will metamorphose from the I who will not want them to enter into the I who wants to let them in.) A milk bottle will descend a flight of basement steps outside, its irregular movement will make me think it controls its descent by its shape. My watch will have stopped at 4.33 a.m. or p.m. I will resolve the music, stamping and lavatory flushing into the party it will be upstairs. I will not know whether I have been in this room an hour, a night, or a day and a half. Then I will remember I am in London, no longer on the run. I will be hungry.

Against the white skin the vein will bluely rise (like a reversed vapour trail on a summer sky), the snake beneath the skin.

Gloriously, like a film of Hiroshima in technicolour when you're drunk or an avalanche of bells down the silence of the night when you're in a van accelerating away from a shop you've just robbed the meaning of the words will go off in my miserable life – I love you – spoken in this filthy room unexpectedly to me, (and as I will hear them the thought that will never leave me that my world is not worth living in will change ['Don't – ' the grey silent moon is invaded by noise and colour and I return to earth ' – shoot!'] into the thought that this is more than I could ever deserve), and I will be the winner of a beautiful prize and the prize will be myself – new, alive, radiant.

What I will have been earning in prison with every stitch (eight mailbag stitches to the inch) I was forced to inject in cloth for injecting this ... That's what this shot of heroin will be like. There will be no cure. How will I cure being well. 'Drugs cure normal life, stop you feeling ill,' I will say to myself.

I will feel as if I was standing in a cell in solitary confinement for the rest of my life completely filled with the meaning of the phrase, 'I am going mad.'

I will take my lino cutter from my case (I've got to hand it to myself) and poised over my wrist will begin to spin, a whirlpool of memories, thoughts, feelings, sensations; no longer a person who could stab. I will look at myself in the mirror and say to myself, 'It was only a feeling, like any other feeling.' Sink. The words will be like revolving suds above. But a feeling will not be like any other feeling or I would feel the same continuously!

I am talking to you I will say to myself.

Being logical will not be logical enough, being beautiful will not be beautiful enough; being perfect will be an imperfection!

'Insanity', 'terror', 'infinity', etc. One word after another. Suds.

I feel sorry for you I say to myself I say to myself I say to myself I say to myself I say to myself etc.

This will be a hook. This will be me pulling you towards me. You will be drowning. When I will be dead you will be watching on TV a diver exploring a wreck, the streaming of his bubbles, and you will suddenly realize you have been holding your breath – you will be me. I will feel sorry for you. You will have me to turn to.

In the foyer the night porter will give me five pounds for twenty dollars and inform me it is Saturday.

I will walk sleepily down the street, take a right turn and a left; because of the pills and shot of H manipulating my body as foolish as if I could leave it if I wished (walking through Earls Court with a big grin on its face forever). Ahead of me three men and two girls will get out of a Ford and enter a house where there will be a party on the second floor. I will follow them up the stairs into a dimly-lit room full of standing people.

Nothing will be happening. They will be between tracks of an LP, it will be like a rush hour subway train in a station. A door will open, a man will come out; he will say to me, rolling his eyes, 'They're talking about their trips.' I will go in, some students will be sat around the room, I will sit on a bed between posters of Lenin and Trotsky and presently will be handed a large hash-loaded hand-rolled cigarette. As I will say 'Thanks' four men in dinner jackets will come in unwinding white silk scarves from their necks and easing overcoats off their shoulders. I will step into the vacuum behind them and run down the stairs into the street and round a corner with the joint still alight.

A voice will say, 'Hey man you want to *get* busted there's fuzz crawling *out* the woodwork round here.' It will be a kind voice drawing me to him, I will hand him the joint and he will take a deep drag and smile. It will be the first warm smile directed at me in months. Then I will be hit on the head with a blunt instrument.

My brain will argue its first reaction from the innocent premiss that it would be impossible to be struck from behind – therefore for the previous few minutes I will have been launching upwards and had now met a ceiling. I will have fallen from a great height nearly to the ground before coming to as I will hit it.

I will not have been hit very hard, I will not lose consciousness, as I go down I will think my assailants wouldn't have lasted a week in New York. ('Even when you're attacked and robbed you've got to know the drill – collapse slowly in case they think you're going to hit them back when they'd smash you a second time, finish up on your back so that they can get at your wallet without having to kick you in the stomach to turn you over, keep the eyes shut, nobody likes to be looked at when they're busy robbing.' I will say to Elaine a few hours later.) One of them will unfasten my watch, the other find my five pounds.

When they will have gone I will crawl behind a dustbin, I will be in a mews. A yellow E-type will miss me by a foot. Spinning like roulette wheels its shining spokes will come to rest further down. A man and a beautiful woman will be hatched and go into their homes. I will vomit.

Back in my room I will suck the barrel of my pistol to taste the metal. Later. I will wrap the pistol in a vest and stow it under the toilet bag. I will spin the combination to lock the case, sheathing my sting. 'Would you step this way sir,' I will say to myself pointing at the bed. My bed: a bad landing on weak springs.

The benefit of my last shot will be waning, the room will soon be clocking up another day's charge, my clothes and shoes will be wearing out, I will be poorer by the second. My room will be too small for me, the city will be too large – I will feel enormously small.

Elaine will come and pay me my £200. 'Your last trip kid,' she will say, 'your nerve's busted, and we don't need anybody with your habit.' By gesture, facial expression and movement of her body she will invite me to fuck her. I will say to her, 'Undressing you is going to be like burgling

Harrods.' She will laugh and take her clothes off genuinely disappointed, I will not enjoy it as much as she.

She will not have shut the door and not being hung properly it will swing open as she sits naked on the bed. I will nearly shout 'Shut the fucking door' but it will decline on my mouth into a smile which will be more a snarl to her. I will shut the door. My head will approach hers. It will be my first good look at her and her first good look at me. Look. We will make love. I will stand up, she will not move on the bed where she will have come to rest in an irregular arrangement of arms and legs and torso. I will have wanted the door of tense sensation where my skin met hers to have opened for me to pass through into the warmth of pleasure. Zero. It will have been a desperate hope. I will be by the sink, I will imagine picking up the tumbler and throwing it at her, seeing it miss her beautiful body and shatter over her, her widowing confetti!

I will lean close to the mirror and stick out my tongue, viper, which will be yellow.

I will imagine opening my mouth and a long scream unreeling out of it, an ugly snake of sound winding down the corridor, up and down the stairs at the end of the corridor and along the corridors above and below the second floor, into every room of the hotel.

I will look at her (I will feel like a science-fiction character who has been invaded by alien intelligences – she will seem like a member of another species), I will look at her.

Elaine will tell me as a favour that she has orders to report me to the police. She will say, 'If you could kick your habit you could be anything you wanted. But you'll never feel it, because if you could feel it you wouldn't have to try to.' 'Could I marry you?' I will ask. 'Yes,' she will say and leave the room.

I will feel I ought to check out of the hotel, check into another. But I will be so depressed I will think shooting myself would not drain away the depression. 'Drowning men see their whole lives as they die,' I will remember that phrase and think of Brian Jones. I will be immersed in my mind. I will have to listen more carefully.

I will be on my back with an inexhaustible running commentary going on as if I had an audience, but the audience will be down to one, myself, myself about to switch off. 'Don't miss next week's exciting epi – ' an ambulance, its driver whirling the aural lasso of its siren about its flasher will race down the road outside, but though I will escape it the siren will be like a whisk through my mind. I will be looking at the wall six inches from my eyes and at my hand, the indecipherable lines on its palm and fingers. Through the wall another portion of human blancmange will be slopping round, washing, tidying, undressing, masturbating – functioning normally. And through the wall at the other side also, and above me and below me, millions of them – functioning normally.

I will plead guilty now and be finally where I belong, officially 'in the wrong', a lump of human freight to be shunted for a few more months from cell to cell, helplessly.

By day from the exercise yard I will see a sky crisscrossed by jets.

At night, over me in my cell in Wormwood Scrubs the sound of a goods train from Willesden will roll slowly, truck by truck.

I will feel flat.

That fucking maniac – he will have only me to turn to.

. . . Gulf – you.

Anthony Burton

Crrrrrrkkkkkk

Friday, August the twenty-first

A day which began inauspiciously – the weather predict-
ably damp, and the temperature depressingly down. Having
accustomed myself to spending the morning in bed, in order
to nurse my far from hardy constitution, I was rather later
than most in becoming aware of the singular occurrence
which was to shatter the bucolic calm of Compton Mallett.
The event itself would appear to have happened between
the hours of ten and eleven a.m. The doubt concerning the
actual timing of the event will cause no surprise to those
cognisant with the ways of the English agricultural
employee. However, as the precise timing is largely im-
material to the narrative which I am setting down, the
reader will I trust forgive this one note of dubiety in an
account which can otherwise be verified by personal observation.

Let us assume then that the time is between ten and eleven, and consider the aforementioned occurrence, which
was so to change the disposition, both physical and mental,
of my pastoral neighbours. At this time, there descended
into a crop of wheat, a metallic vessel of some seventy feet in
length, with a diameter at its widest part of approximately
fifteen feet. This, as can be imagined, occasioned a great deal
of speculation in the village, and theories to explain the unexpected arrival were not difficult to discover. The landlord
of the 'Pig and Pheasant' offered the view that the missile
had inadvertently appeared in Compton Mallett as a result

of a navigational error. The error was attributed variously to the Soviet Union, the United States, the Welsh and the Ministry of Fuel and Power. Thus, although there remained differences regarding the exact source, the devotees of that hostelry were able to reach some measure of agreement, and to present a reasonably united front to the habitués of the 'Hog and Halibut', the alternative source of refreshment in the village. The latter held tenaciously to the view that the event was in some way connected with electronic entertainment – an elaborate jest in which hidden cameras had been cunningly placed to record every grimace and imbecilic remark of any of the local yeomanry foolhardy enough to wish to investigate. The philosophy of the Halibuteans could be summarized as one of laissez-faire, and, equally, the Pheasantries, conditioned by a lifetime of avoidance of men from all Ministries, favoured massive indifference. Amidst this surge of inaction, there appeared one dissident voice – that of George Crafton, who protested most vociferously that action was essential and, indeed, a duty. This unheralded interruption to the community life must be removed, and suitable steps taken to deal immediately with whosoever should prove to be responsible for the outrage. This unexpected show of civic responsibility was received with indifference, and the cynical were heard to comment that Mr Crafton's enthusiasm could be readily explained by his ownership of the wheatfield which had been laid low by the intruder's arrival.

I viewed this debate with impartiality, but, being possessed with a deal more foresight than my co-habitants took it upon myself to chronicle these events with scientific detachment, certain that the circumstances would hardly fail to lead to a situation where my own intellectual attributes would be required. However, I resolved not to be forced into any precipitate action, nor indeed to be forced into any position where direct and prolonged physical activity might be deemed necessary. For a man of my disposition, reasons must be found, both cogent and pressing, before I may even contemplate action of a forceful nature. Even should such a situation arise, I have always felt the necessity of ensuring that any such action should be swift and elegant, and free from the more mundane characteristics of this workaday world. Whilst prepared to cut the Gordian knot, I am loath to clean the Augean stables.

For the moment, I shall therefore be concerned merely with the role of reporter, reserving to myself the role of saviour, which I shall assume at such time as the local populace shall have reduced the whole situation to one of characteristic chaos.

Saturday, August the twenty-second

Very little change – opinion flows aimlessly, whilst the undercurrent of Crafton gathers momentum. The object of all our curiosities remains motionless and inert.

Sunday, August the twenty-third

The Reverend Charles H. Spendwick touched briefly on our visitation in the course of a sermon on the text 'Few and evil have the days of the years of my life been' – a text which, not surprisingly, he was referring to the congregation rather than his blameless self. The reference to our visitor was however so couched and so beset by apt quotation, mainly in Greek, that the listeners were able either to ignore it, or take it as confirmation of their own preconceptions as they chose.

Monday, August the twenty-fourth

A day of decisions and miracles indeed – an extraordinary general meeting of the Village Council was called for 3 p.m. This was a decision of some magnitude and previously had only been taken twice within living memory; firstly to deliberate the action necessary to replace the roof of the Village Hall removed in the course of a tempest of unusual severity, and secondly to muster a team of firewatchers to deal with any possible aerial bombardment of the hamlet during the recent hostilities. Yet this Extraordinary General Meeting was destined never to take place.

George Crafton, the increasingly irate owner of the mal-treated crops, decided to take matters into his own hands. He was a large and, truth to tell, somewhat flabby individ-ual. The multitude of broken purple veins which spread from his nose to proliferate on his cheeks spoke less of ex-posure to the elements than of overindulgence in rough cider, brewed in large quantities by his equally corpulent wife. The loss of his crops was deemed by him as something in the nature of a personal insult, and, encouraged by his wife and her beverage, he stumbled into action. Unable to resist the opportunity of displaying his new-found sense of impor-tance, he began his crusade with calls at both the 'Pig and Pheasant' and the 'Hog and Halibut', where he further re-inforced his courage and fuddled his senses. Consequently, when he eventually moved off towards his field, armed with pickaxe and twelve-bore shotgun, he was followed at a reasonable distance by virtually every mobile member of the village. All this I watched from my bedroom window through a pair of powerful field-glasses – as a life-long suf-ferer from a number of debilitating nervous disorders, I felt that no good purpose could be served by my mingling with the inebriated throng.

Eventually the whole party arrived. The spectators settled themselves comfortably around the periphery of the field to observe the ensuing entertainment. Crafton marched boldly across the field, brandishing his weapons – slowing visibly as the distance between himself and the shimmering capsule diminished. Spurred on by the ribaldry of the crowd, he eventually reached the object of his malice, whereupon he tapped tentatively upon its outer surface. Receiving no res-ponse, he began to belabour the metal with his pickaxe, mouthing the while. Fortunately, my distance from the scene prevented my sensibility from being injured by ac-tually hearing what was said, but my imagination was suffi-ciently strong for me to be pained by the thought of it. The climax of this physical and vocal activity was swift and startling – and the reader will I am sure excuse me if I pause a moment both to make one important observation and to gather my strength to describe the occurrence. It is essential that the reader appreciate that to all outward appearance the missile was all of one piece; no crack, aperture or rugosity disturbed the smoothness of the surface. With this in mind, he will be better able to appreciate the horror and surprise with which the event that next occurred impressed itself on the witnesses: the capsule opened. From within the darkness behind the newly-apparent door, an arm appeared – muscular, hirsute and of gigantic proportions, clasped Crafton and withdrew. The door closed. Then, from inside what I shall now describe as the machine, there came a noise, audible even to me at my great distance from the scene. The noise, rendered onomatopoeically, was

CRRRKKK

The crowd remained motionless and silent. The door of the machine reopened, and a creature emerged into the light. He appeared in every way to resemble a man, and as he was totally unclad this was readily ascertainable. In every way that is except in his size. At a modest estimate he was some fourteen feet in height. At the sight of this giant naked man, four of the local maidens fainted clear away – but whether from fear or anticipation I was never able to discern. The creature stood and surveyed the crowd before, politely raising its hand to its mouth, it broke wind and from behind the hand there emerged two large rubber gumboots. There could be no doubt that these represented the mortal remains of George Crafton Esq., lately farmer of this parish.

The locals fled, in many ways the most surprising event of the whole day. I do not believe that in forty-five years' residence in Compton Mallett I had previously seen one citizen move beyond a slow, ambling walk. Yet on this occasion, the agility of even the eldest would not have disgraced an international athletic tournament. The creature watched them depart with apparent indifference, contenting itself with licking its fingers, no doubt with the intention of removing all traces of the unpalatable agricultural footwear. It remained thus for some while, then abruptly turned on its heel, re-entered the machine, and closed the door behind itself.

Having been deprived of all aural communication, with the exception of the one digestive note, I moved from my secluded position to the village green, with the intention of collecting direct comment from the participants in the ungainly rout. The local representative of law and order, Police Constable George Barnes, was torn between attempting to take down the eye-witness accounts of the incident from a multitude of sources, and in admonishing the licensees of the two inns that they should forebear serving alcoholic beverages outside the officially allowed hours. This latter purpose was forestalled by the vicar, who intervened suggesting that an exception might be made in the circumstances; and his heavy breathing and generally perplexed air strongly suggested that he might well be the first to take advantage of any relaxation of the law. When some semblance of order was restored, an informal village meeting was convened in the Village Hall. This was opened by the Chairman of the Council, who began with an unaccustomed firmness of purpose. He suggested, in the strongest terms, that this represented a case which could be best dealt with by the official forces of the law. Constable Barnes could hardly have a better opportunity to bring a culprit to book than was given him at this moment. He had merely to effect an arrest, and the whole matter would have been cleared up to the satisfaction of all. Constable Barnes responded with less than enthusiasm. Whilst he appreciated the trust laid on him, he would be doing less than his duty if he did not point out that there were certain factors in the case which could well be overlooked by anyone less conversant than himself with the intricacies of the law. Firstly, before preferring a charge of murder, it was necessary to produce a body, and one pair of slightly chewed gumboots did not represent an adequate substitute. Secondly, that there had been no witness of the actual slaying of the unfortunate farmer, and that his death must remain a matter of conjecture. He would, however, be prepared to admit that a case did exist for a charge of indecent exposure, which had been hugely evident to all present. A certain amount of friendly, if somewhat coarse, ribaldry greeted these last remarks, and when this had died down, the worthy constable continued his discourse by an expression of sympathy towards the malefactor, who was clearly not of local origin and could therefore not reasonably be expected to be conversant with the local legal position regarding the display of the nether regions of the torso in a public place. Needless to say, I have found it necessary to paraphrase and considerably clarify the officer's own disjointed and somewhat incoherent testimony, in order to save the reader the agony of attempting to thread for himself the labyrinthine prose of the speaker.

The establishment of the non-intervention policy of the official law-enforcement officer mollified the tone of the meeting. After a brusque exchange of comment and question, which absolutely failed to move the gentleman from his entrenched position, it was clear to even the meanest minds present that any action to be taken would have to be the responsibility of some other member of the public. There was little eagerness to accept this role, and the general feeling became evident; that it was the clear duty of the Parish Council to take command of the situation. The Chairman of the Council, Councillor Goodberry, had clearly given the matter his most earnest attention. He rose and addressed the meeting in a voice unstirred by emotion. It was, he suggested, an unfortunate matter that their friend and good neighbour, George Crafton, had met such an untimely end, and sympathies were expressed to the widow. However, he felt that his precipitate action in making a frontal assault on a complete stranger, who had hitherto shown no signs of unfriendliness, nor indeed of anything else, could be considered as having contributed in large manner to his downfall. It was his opinion that a party of peace should be despatched the very next day to the stranger to

Anthony Burton

welcome him to the village, which only three years previously
had been appointed by the British Travel and Holiday
Association, the most friendly village in East Wiltshire
(Class B, under 5,000 inhabitants). This motion was
accepted with alacrity, and after a few words from the vicar
on charity, the announcement of the names of the raffle
winners and the cricket team for the following Saturday,
the meeting dispersed.

Tuesday, August the twenty-fifth

The following day was bright and sunny, and it was in an
idyllic setting that the welcoming delegation formed on the
green at ten-thirty.

At the head of the procession was the Prize Silver Band,
instruments burnished, resplendent in Sunday serge, their
crimson caps with their shiny plastic peaks, lending the
quasi-military air, which is always considered so essential
to the production of band music. The varied purples of
their faces clashed rather unfortunately with the colour of
the headwear, yet added its own touch of gaiety to the morning. Immediately behind them came the members of the
Council, with the Chairman in full regalia at their head. The
main procession formed the rear, and consisted of representatives of the local organizations: twenty-seven members
of the Women's Institute, fourteen representatives of the
Home Guard, who had unfortunately never received their
official notification of disbandment, seventeen Boy Scouts,
eleven Wolf Cubs and nineteen Brownies. The whole village followed at a reasonable distance, myself amongst them.
Constable Barnes acted as shepherd to the motley flock, as
they moved off at a respectful pace towards the machine
and its inhabitant.

The procession shortly reached the field, where they discovered the creature sat outside his machine, idly picking
at his teeth with wheat stems. The sight of the teeth and the
unpleasant memories that they evoked caused a certain
wavering in the ranks. Furthermore, his form of dress, or

rather lack of it, was the same as on his last appearance. It was deemed seemly for the female members of the party to be escorted back to the village in the interests of modesty. The remainder after a certain amount of jostling for the rear moved in orderly fashion across the field. A few yards from the creature the procession halted, the Prize Silver Band formed up in twos, and the Chairman was admitted through the ranks to deliver his address.

He commenced in a high falsetto, quite unlike his normal base baritone, so evident at choral evensong. After a short fit of coughing, he regained control of his vocal mechanism, and began reading his welcoming address from a crumpled sheet of paper. The reading was not one of the higher flights of oratory, the Chairman losing his place three times in the first sentence, and twice dropping his notes. The creature listened, however, quietly and politely, and with a gentlemanly reserve that I could not help but admire. The Chairman and his speech berame progressively more confused, until in an attempt to recover his rapidly waning dignity, he raised his hat in the air and bravely called 'God Save the Queen'. This was the signal for the instrumentalists to commence their rendition of the National Anthem.

Over the years my ears have become accustomed to the cacophony which, to the best of my knowledge, remains unique in the musical world. I have indeed known outwardly sane and reasonable men react in the most alarming fashion to the assault on the eardrums of our worthy musicians, yet nothing could compare to the violence of the reactions of the creature to this affront to his hearing. In one bound he was upon the players

CRRRKKK

eight shiny instruments lay ownerless on the ground. The resulting panic may be imagined, and I must with shame confess that I too moved with something more than my accustomed speed. Looking at intervals over my shoulder I caught glimpses of the mayhem which was in progress.

The engorgement of one entire Prize Silver Band appeared to have far from allayed the creature's appetite, and one sound could be heard amongst the cries and scattering feet.

CRRRKKK

I turned in time to see the chain of office follow its owner into the maw

CRRRKKK

A young Boy Scout met a fate never dreamed of by Baden Powell even during the darkest days of Mafeking

CRRRKKK

The arm of the law was the last I was ever to see of Police Constable Barnes, who that day answered the final call of duty and disappeared bicycle clips and all

Crrrkkk

Crrrkkk

Crrrkkk

the sound swept away into the distance, as I fled up the driveway of my house, and collapsed into my study.

The unaccustomed excitement had quite exhausted me, and as I had feared, my excursion among the fields served to bring on my asthma. My day of suffering was complete.

Wednesday, August the twenty-sixth

I felt quite unable to arise before lunch, and spent the morning sipping beef tea, considering the events of the previous day. There could no longer be any doubt of the total incompetence of the local peasantry when faced with a situation of such novelty, and the time had clearly arrived for intellect to banish dumb instinct from the stage. Their well-meaning but misguided attempts to deal with the creature, who for convenience I had now christened Cyclop, had failed due to their unimaginative offering of violence. The late Mr Crafton had offered violence in a crudely physical fashion, by battering at Cyclop's door with a pickaxe; hardly an action likely to endear a stranger. The violence to the sensibilities offered by the Compton Mallett Prize Silver Band was, if anything, yet more hideous to any creature of culture, which my observation of Cyclop during the welcoming address had indicated him to be. I resolved therefore to spend some time observing the habits of Cyclop, to ascertain how he employed himself when left to his own devices. This observation occupied me for the whole of the afternoon, excepting only for one half-hour for tea. During all this time Cyclop followed a peaceful and purely pastoral mode of life. True, he assuaged his hunger at the expense of one Hereford, but otherwise seemed content to contemplate nature in as quiet a fashion as would delight the most rigorous of the Romantic poets. By the time that I was ready to retire for the night I had formulated a modus operandi for the morrow.

Thursday, August the twenty-seventh

I confess to a feeling of some intellectual stimulation at the prospect of establishing contact with the bizarre Cyclop. (I have made a mental reservation, that I must avoid using the term in his presence, lest he has had the benefit of a classical education.)

I have prepared the lawn for afternoon tea on a suitably gargantuan scale. Spode, for all its excellencies, would hardly meet the occasion, and I have been forced to sacrifice some elegance in the cause of practicality. Tureens have had to replace teacups, platters saucers, and for the brewing I have followed the simple adage of a pound per person and one for the pot. The scene, in short, is set for a meeting of gentlemanly minds, and all that now remains is to establish my desire to make the acquaintance of Cyclop, and bid him welcome to the modest feast. I have decided against any direct approach. Having suffered so greatly from the inroads into his privacy made by what I can only assume to be my late neighbours, Cyclop will hardly be in a mood to receive fresh visitors, other than internally.

Anthony Burton

After a light lunch, I again retired to my bedroom, where I settled myself at the window overlooking Cyclop and his metallic home. Steadily I waved a large white pocket handkerchief in his direction, maintaining the while a welcoming smile, and beckoning occasionally with my free hand. The white handkerchief I consider to be a particularly fortunate touch – white being a colour universally recognized as signifying pacific intentions, and a clean pocket handkerchief giving both by its intimacy and cleanliness a sense of domesticity and propriety. I have patiently maintained this activity for something approaching an hour, and have at last been gratified by a response. Cyclop has returned my salutation, and I have every hope that he can be induced to call. The excitement has been a little overpowering, and I am therefore taking this opportunity to repair to my chronicle before resuming the vigil.

Success indeed, as I distinctly hear distant steps – ah, what amazements might there not be to record this evening.

Th. Aug 27: Ref.: inquiry 875/4285/b

3.45 p.m. Entered house as requested. Appeared deserted. Report of large figure heading in easterly direction. Enclosed diary apparently relevant. On approaching drive, loud noise heard.

CRRRRRRRKKK

Anthony Burton

Mister Newcome Runs for the 8.35 Every Morning Except for Weekends

Newcome's coming down the track now. Watch him go. Go. Go. What fantastic speed. Faster than the speed of light. Is it a bird? Is it a plane? No, it's Superman!

UP, UP AND AWAY

Mild mannered office worker John Newcome changes into the mighty Superman, possessed of superhuman powers. Zoom. Up to the twelfth floor. Hover outside window of lady's lav. Here comes the beautiful Miss Creasy, swashing her tits. Down with her knickers and a brief enchanting view. Surely not? Yes. Yes. Yes. She's paddling her fingers in the fleshpots, rolling and moaning. This is a job for

SUPERMAN

With his magical, dissolving action, Superman flows effortlessly through the brickwork. Pops up miraculously in the Ladies Lav.

Madam your troubles are over.

Off from the lav bowl and on to the floor. Skirts round her waist. Flips her blouse and out pops a booby.

Oh. Superman, Superman to my rescue.

How does he ever get out of that stupid costume. Does he have a zip fly and Y-fronts.

STEEL ERECTORS WANTED.
APPLY WITHIN.

Agonies for the man of steel.

NO EXIT

Up, up and away. Superman, faster than the speed of light. Superman wets his pants. Superman wets his pants.

Eight twenty six. I'm buggered already. Walk ten yards. Run ten yards. Walk ten yards. Run ten yards.

One, two, three, four, five, six, seven, eight, nine, ten. Onetwothreefourfivesixseveneightnineten.

One, two, three, four, five, six, seven, eight, nine, ten. Onetwothreefourfivesixseveneightnineten.

If I one run two I'm three covering four more five ground six because seven I'm eight taking nine longer ten

Onetwothreefourfivesixseveneightnineten strides.

Old Boy Scout trick. Stops you getting puffed. You can go for hours like this. It says here. It's bloody near killing me. Good morning troop. Dib dib dib, dob, dob, dob. Good morning Scoutmaster.

I can't see it. I suppose it's all those plump little arses. Brightest and best of the sons of the morning. Exceptional opportunities for men under twenty-one. Here grab a handful.

I just don't see it.

Good morning troop.

Scoutmaster.

Yes, Mister Jones.

There are terrible rumours. These aren't real scouts.

We'll soon see about that Mister Jones. Off we go troops to the showers.

No, no sir. We can't go to the showers.

Ho, ho, ho. Throw them all in.

Just as I thought. Transvestite lesbians. They're wearing nylon uniforms and nothing else. Once they get in the water they become transparent. Look at all those stuck-up nipples.

Now girls I'm going to give you a lecture.

Yes, Mister Scoutmaster.

I'm pretty broadminded, but the Boy Scouts is no place for a girl. And take those wet things off, you'll all catch your death of colds. Fourteen bare bodies. They've kept their climbing boots on and their knee socks. It's time to be *real* girls. Triumph for the troop. They've learned the terror of their ways. Red troop leader sat astride, bouncing ecstatically.

Little girl cries.

There, there dear, you can be a troop leader one day. Come a little closer and I'll play with you. There, that's better isn't it. Jesus Christ, eight twenty nine.

The starter's got his pistol raised, and they're away. Newcome's gone straight to the front. He's setting a cracking pace. Surely he can't keep this up. The rest of the field's lagging behind, waiting for him to crack. What's the time for the first lap, Dick? Fifty seconds. This is amazing. He's still going. The crowd are rising to this brilliant new runner. There's no one else in the race. It's an amazing start for a mile. I've never seen anything like it. Now we'll get his time at the end of the second lap. Fifty seconds. This is incredible. The third lap. Exactly fifty seconds. (No one knows of my secret breathing and heart beat control methods, ha, ha.) He's on his final lap now, and still keeping up this fantastic pace. The rest of the runners are nowhere near him. The crowd are cheering him on

NEW COME NEW COME COME COME COME

He's coming off the last bend now. He's finished. Another lap of fifty seconds. Newcome's run a mile in four fives are twenty that's two hundred three sixes are eighteen that's one hundred and eighty is three minutes plus twenty three minutes twenty seconds. This is unbelievable. Everyone's crowding round him and still he's showing no signs of strain.

Can I have your autograph? You're fantastic. A few

words for the viewers. This is my card. Call round at the apartment at eight.

Good evening, you asked me to call round.

Come in. Do you mind waiting while I change. Fix yourself a drink.

Hope I didn't keep you.

She's wearing the same dress. But she's taken off her stockings. What does it mean, ha ha?

Come and sit by me.

Kisses. Run hand up leg. Ha ha. Just as I thought. She went to take off her underwear. Pulls down zip. All is revealed. She's shaved her crutch. Oh! its smooth on the thick white carpet for less than half a crown. Look where you're going, can't you. Jesus Christ it's eighty thirty one.

You're late again, Newcome. You're fired.

Headlines in the evening paper.

OFFICE WORKER JOHN NEWCOME
FOILS ARMED THIEVES

Newcome it's the chairman here. I've just seen the paper. Why didn't you tell us that was why you were late?

I didn't get a chance sir. I was kicked straight out.

The fools. Come back tomorrow we've got a new job for you. Five thousand a year and a company car. We need men like you. Ha, ha. And a five thousand reward.

Pay off the mortgage, that leaves three thousand eight hundred from five thousand two thousand two hundred.

I booked for the Bahamas dear, and the Chairman's asked us round tonight. He's throwing a party.

Damn niggers ought to be sent back to Africa. Ignorant savages. I don't think you've met my wife, sir.

Georgina Umgabada the most beautiful black girl in the world in her million coloured dazzling sari.

She has a Ph.D. in nuclear physics and speaks ten languages, sir. Collapse of stout party.

The trouble is if you run the train's always fucking late. We regret to announce that owing to a signal failure at

Little Puddleton in the Ooze, the eight thirty five to Victoria will be approximately twenty minutes late.

Eight thirty six and you arrive sweating like a pig.

Course it's gone. Went right on the dot.

Eight thirty three. If I get to the shop in one minute and I get straight over the road and don't get stuck waiting for the traffic. That means eighty thirty four and a bit in the booking hall. On to the platform. In comes the train. All aboard and away we go donkey riding, donkey riding.

What's this? A nun's convention in the booking hall. Sorry sister. Shove it mother. With one leap he bounds over the amazed crowd.

UP, UP AND AWAY

Ha, ha. You're not a nun. You're Count Von Spiegelfluffen. Oh, Superman, you saved us. Come and sample our dirty habits. Ha ha.

Sod this silly costume.

SOGGY WET SUPERKNICKERS STRIKES AGAIN.

Why the hell doesn't she get up earlier. Every fucking morning. Burn your bloody tongue on the coffee and run all the way to the bloody station. Every fucking morning. Crash. Take that you slut.

MILD-MANNERED OFFICE WORKER RUNS AMOK. BEATS WIFE TO PULP

Sorry I'm late, sir. But I killed my wife sir. It won't happen again sir.

That's all right Newcome, just make sure it doesn't.

One minute, sixty seconds. For Christ's sake get out of my way. Ten, eleven twelve.

Pay at the other end.

I've got a season ticket, inspector. Not worth trying.

Sixpenny from the machine. Pay the other end.

Here it comes.

Matter of life and death, inspector. I'm having a baby.

That's it.
Good god.
Eight thirty five.
Shit.
I'm on.
Oh, shit.
It's not bloody worth it.
Oh shit.
Could I borrow your iron lung sir, sir, ha ha.
Oh shit.
Sod this for a lark. I sound like a worn out pump.

Well, come on. Get the fucking thing moving. I didn't nearly kill myself just to sit staring at the bloody platform. Holé.

One across: Instrument for a performer. Nine letters.

Biographical Notes

Penelope Gilliatt

has written two novels, *One by One* and *A State of Change*, and one outstanding collection of short stories: *What's it Like Out?*, about which the famous American short story writer, Jean Stafford, said 'all the stories are brilliant, but some are more amazingly so than others', and which made publishing history by selling out in its first hardback edition. Formerly film critic of the *Observer*, she now works for the *New Yorker* writing film criticism and short stories. She also writes film scripts; her latest, an original for John Schlesinger, is entitled 'Bloody Sunday'. The stories in this volume, with others, will be published shortly in book form by Secker & Warburg and *What's it Like Out?* will soon be appearing in Penguins.

Benedict Kiely

was born in 1919 in County Tyrone, Ireland. He is a graduate of the National University of Ireland and of University College, Dublin and has been visiting professor and writer in residence at four American Universities. He has written eight novels, of which the latest is *Dogs Enjoy the Morning*, one collection of short stories, and three non-fiction books. Literary editor of a Dublin daily newspaper for fourteen years, he is now a Council Member of the Irish Academy of Letters, a member of the Academic Committee of the American-Irish Foundation and a regular contributor to periodicals on both sides of the Atlantic. He is married, with four children, and lives in Dublin.

Biographical Notes

Andrew Travers

was born in 1944 near Manchester. He read Philosophy at Bristol University and started writing short stories while he was there. He is currently working on a novel to be called *Millionaire*. This is his first appearance in print.

Anthony Burton

was born in Yorkshire in 1934, read Chemistry at Leeds University and worked in publishing in London for eight years before leaving to write full time. Since 1968 he has published *A Programmed Guide to Office Warfare* and has completed a sequel *The Jones Report* which will be published later this year. He has written two original screenplays, both scheduled for production, and is currently writing and co-directing a cartoon film about idiotic Victorian inventions entitled *The Grand Mechanical and Optical Eidopheusikon*. He is also working on a novel.

More about Penguins and Pelicans

Penguinews, which appears every month, contains details of all the new books issued by Penguins as they are published. From time to time it is supplemented by *Penguins in Print*, which is a complete list of all books published by Penguins which are in print (There are well over three thousand of these.)

A specimen copy of *Penguinews* will be sent to you free on request, and you can become a subscriber for the price of the postage. For a year's issues (including the complete lists) please send 4s. if you live in the United Kingdom, or 8s. if you live elsewhere. Just write to Dept EP, Penguin Books Ltd, Harmondsworth, Middlesex, enclosing a cheque or postal order, and your name will be added to the mailing list.

Other volumes in the Penguin Modern Stories series are listed on the following page.

Note: *Penguinews* and *Penguins in Print* are not available in the U.S.A. or Canada

Penguin Modern Stories

There are today so few serious publications devoted to the short story that there is no need, in introducing *Penguin Modern Stories*, to say more than that we believe in the short story, know that a great many of the best contemporary writers are working in this form, and look forward to publishing many well-known authors as well as introducing many new ones in this quarterly series. All these stories are published here for the first time in this country.

*Volume 1 contains stories by William Sansom, Jean Rhys, David Plante, and Bernard Malamud.

*Volume 2 contains stories by John Updike, Sylvia Plath, and Emanuel Litvinoff.

Volume 3 contains stories by Philip Roth, Margaret Drabble, Jay Neugeboren, and Giles Gordon.

Volume 4 contains stories by Sean O'Faolain, Nadine Gordimer, Isaac Babel, and Shiva Naipaul.

Not for sale in the U.S.A. or Canada
*Not for sale in the U.S.A.